Choices

Tales for Teens

"I ain't what I ought to be. I ain't what I'm going to be, but I'm not what I was."

Erik
Erikson on
adolescence

EBONY

Why in the fuck hadn't mama stopped at three or four like most normal people? No, her dumb ass had to have eleven. Damn! Ebony thought as she paced back and forth from the alley on 4th to the corner in the pouring rain. Not only was it raining but the weather had changed.

An early winter was forecasted and it sure as shit felt like it was here already. She wasn't sure if it was just the freezing rain or if it was hail. All she knew as she pulled the wool coat up around her neck was that it was too cold to be out there trying to flag down a trick.

In the six months since Ms. Lena had passed things had grown progressively worse. First, the city had confiscated the house saying back taxes were due and all the grooming Ms. Lena had done so Ebony could take over now seemed all for nothing. Lena had done her best to ingratiate the young woman with all the right people but truth of the matter was they still viewed her as just another young Black prostitute prone to violence, sex, drugs and all the things that they didn't want in their little one horse cracker town. So, here she was in a totally unfamiliar place, a place she hardly knew.

Ebony started off in Ms. Lena's house and knew little else. She had never been a common streetwalker. Ms. Lena's was a high class brothel where local politicians, businessmen, the police chief and other notable persons in and around Raeford would stop on their way home from work to take a peek, have a drink, and maybe even enjoy the company of one or two of the girls before they went home to their wives. And never once did Ebony feel threatened while in Ms. Lena's employ but in the six months since she'd been in the streets, she'd been robbed twice, beaten up badly enough to be hospitalized for three days and arrested so many times she'd lost count. The money was considerably less too. At Ms. Lena's if a customer wanted to spend the night the minimum was a thousand dollars. Now she was lucky to get fifty dollars from a trick and the only way she could look to make a hundred or more was if she rifled some drunks pockets who'd fallen asleep somewhere or was in a drunken stupor. She'd saved her money just as Ms. Lena had advised but with ten brothers and sisters always needing something and her not making the money she was accustomed to her savings was slowly starting to dwindle.

Ebony tried to hold on to the few regulars she'd acquired while at Ms. Lena's and tried to accrue a few more and keep in contact with the remaining girls that were still in the area but most of them had gone their separate ways when Ms. Lena died. All that was except Carrie and she could hardly be counted on. It seemed like she was trying her best to drink herself to death and no matter what Ebony did or said in the way of encouragement Carrie seemed hell bent on killing herself.

And no matter what Ebony did to upright the sinking ship that was fast becoming her life it seemed that with each day she'd sink a little lower until tonight when she stood freezing in the pouring rain hoping, praying that someone would stop at least long enough where she could jump in for a few minutes and grab some heat and get the chill of the freezing rain out of her bones. As bad as it sounded a job at the turkey plant almost seemed a reasonable alternative but with her record for loitering and prostitution there wasn't even the remotest possibility of that and she was barely nineteen. Her thoughts were jumbled as she sought answers to deliver her from the malaise she now found herself engulfed in when a navy blue sedan slowly pulled over to the curb.

"What's up lady?"

Peering in Ebony watched as the young brown skinned man smiled at her through the cracked window. Ebony noticed the platinum necklace, which hung from his neck and the matching bracelet as he unlocked the door and pushed it open.

"Get in," he said beckoning her to get in.

"Damn G. It's certainly good to see you. I ain't see you since school. What's it been about two years?" Ebony said glad for the warmth of the car as she rubbed her hands together in an effort to generate some heat.

"Yeah. We was in the same homeroom. What was ol' girl's name?"

"Mrs. Robeson."

"Yeah, she was something. She loved her some Ebony Mitchell. I remember she'd wait for you everyday before she took roll. She used to always wait a few extra minutes saying how you wasn't like the rest of us. How we could all learn something from you. Used to say how you was going to make something of yourself because despite all the responsibility and pressure of having to help with the raising of eight or nine brothers and sisters you still manage to make it to school every day and were a good student. We all used to laugh under our breath but no one would ever say anything because the woman had it all worked out but we all knew why you was late. But nobody ever had the nerve to bust her bubble or tell her the truth about why you was really late even though most of us knew that you'd be out earning til the first bell rang," G said laughing softly.

"Thanks for not telling her the reason why," Ebony said still shaking.

"Wasn't none of my business to say nothing but when you dropped out later that year that old woman was really crushed. I mean she was really crushed. Came in and told us some ol' lie about how you had to quit school to take care of your sick mother and how the responsibility was now all on you to raise them younguns. When she finished she almost had me ready to take up a fund on yo' behalf," G said laughing again.

G's voice was and had always been warm and friendly. And like he said he was one of the few who knew how Ebony rolled but he had never been condescending or judgmental when it came to her and wasn't so now and perhaps that was one of the reasons he'd always been cool with her. They'd even blown a few trees together and sniffed a little coke on occasion and enjoyed each others company but had never really gotten to hang out since each of them was old beyond their years, and caught up in heir own thing. G. always dreamed of going to New York and doing his own thing. He used to tell her how his fam was more or less running things uptown and in the Bronx and soon as he had enough paper he was headed that way. And not two months after Ebony dropped out so had he and without saying goodbye he'd done just that. At the time it was all just talk but here it was two years later and here was G in a brand new whip looking good as hell with his butter Tims, Evisu jeans, that spelled money and shirt of Egytian silk with platinum necklace and bracelet to match. It now became obvious to her that it hadn't all been just talk.

Pulling the dark blue Beamer slowly over to the curb G turned and smiled at Ebony.

"You didn't believe me when I told you I was going to New York to join the fam did you E?"

"I see it wasn't all just talk like the rest of these niggas around here," she said still shaking.

"You still cold?" G said turning up the heat. "Hold on I've got just the thing for you," he said sliding his hand under the seat and pulling out a pint of Henney. "Here hit this one time. It should take the chill away."

Ebony reached for the bottle, twisted the cap off and took a sip before capping the bottle and passing it back to the young man. As the liquor began to warm her insides she looked at G even closer and wondered how as cute and nice as he was she'd ever let him slip away.

"Go ahead. You keep it. It's awfully cold out there and I can't see it getting any warmer anytime soon," he said still smiling before reaching into his pocket and pulling out a small cellophane wrapper. The Hennessey took the chill away and her mind was immediately clear and her thoughts went straight to the fact that it was getting late and she still hadn't picked up her first trick. G. handed her the cellophane wrapper. Ebony took it and scooped up enough of the white powder to get a good rush. She then fed her other nostril.

"Damn G what is that shit? It burns like hell." Ebony said rubbing her nose.

"Oh I thought you knew," he laughed. "Most people taste the shit before they put it up their nose. That's some of the best boy in New York City.

My uncle gets it from the Dominicans where he buys his coke. We don't sell it. It's just for recreational use. Breaks up the monotony is all. I know you've sniffed boy before?" G asked somewhat inquisitively.

Before Ebony could answer she opened the car door leaned over and let her insides erupt.

"I guess that answered that," G. replied. Handing her a tissue from the glove compartment Ebony gladly accepted the Kleenex and straightened up. The heroin was slowly taking affect and her eyes slowly drooped 'til they closed. She felt a warmth she'd never known before. She was soaring now and everything that was wrong suddenly seemed all right. She no longer worried about her siblings and their needs or the fact that she was damn near out of money. No, she was at peace for the first time in as long as she could remember and she liked it.

G. couldn't know what she was thinking but the genuine concern showed in his face.

"Yeah, baby thanks. I'm good. Real good. This is my first time doing H but it's cool, real cool."

"Don't let it be anything but another new experience. This shit ain't nothing to play with. "Here hit this one time," he said handing her another cellophane wrapper.

"What's this?"

"Your favorite. Well it used to be your favorite."

"If it's coke it still is," she said opening the package and sniffing before passing it back to G.

"That will even the high out and stop you from nodding."

"Ooh that's good."

"Only the best for my baby," G said staring at Ebony's legs. There was never any doubt that he was attracted to Ebony. He always had been. They'd just never taken the time to let it happen but the first person G sought was Ebony on his return home. He'd spent many a lonely night walking those Harlem Streets pumping his poison and thinking of Ebony. Now at last, he had a chance to show her just how he'd come up in the game.

"Wanna grab a room?"

"Wish I could honey but I can't. I gotta work."

"How much you charging a night baby? Last time I was here and you were working for Ms. Lena I think the going rate was a grand a night. I wanted you bad back then but I was in no shape. You were out of my league. What would a night with you have cost me back then?"

"A night at Ms. Lena's would have probably cost you a grand or better," Lena smiled as the coke and heroin pulsed through putting her in a mellow sort of melancholy mood. Not even the fact that she had the world on her shoulders and should have been working instead of lounging with G bothered her now.

"Wow! I always thought you were the shit but I had no idea that's what kind of cheddar you were clockin'."

"Yeah, everything was lovely when I was working for the old woman."

"So, what would it cost me now if I were to ask to spend a night with you? I mean I don't think you've lost anything. In fact, I really think you look better now than when I last saw you. Real talk. But you are out here walking the streets now and everybody knows that a common streetwalker ain't commanding the same kind of a money that a high class call girl would. I'm not saying that I think you're common in any way E. but I just gotta watch my dough. You know what I'm sayin'?"

"No offense taken and I'm not even gonna give you a price baby. You want to get a room and spend the night with me. Then we can do that but in the morning I want you to pay me what I'm worth. Is that a fair deal?"

"Sounds good to me love. And when we get finished conducting our business in the morning I want to sit down and talk to you. On the real. I have a business proposition you might be interested in," G said handing

Ebony the cellophane wrapper. "Here baby you keep this. My gift to you."

G pulled the car up to the front of the Marriot and left the car running as he got out and walked to the hotel lobby. Ebony wondered if she were making a mistake leaving the price open bad as she needed money. But thinking back she had known G most, if not all of her life and he had always been straight up and was one of the few brothers who had never jerked her or done anything to cause her any harm whatsoever. These last few months out in the streets had made her skeptical of almost everybody but fear was a good thing and she would have been stupid if she hadn't even considered being ripped off. And naive she wasn't.

Ebony opened the wrapper and found huge chunks of cocaine. There had to be at least three grams or three hundred dollars worth of coke there and the shit was damn near pure. She could put at least a two on it and triple her money. That was close to a thousand dollars. She was sure he'd expect her to party with him but there was no way in hell she was going to sniff all of this. No, she'd sniff just enough to be sociable and save the rest to sell to her respective clients and the other girls out there on the street.

G returned five minutes later a wide smile spread across his face.

"Got us the best room in the house. But let's go to the hotel lounge and grab a couple of drinks first. They have a nice little boutique right off from the lobby. Maybe you can pick up a bathing suit and we can jump into the pool and then the Jacuzzi. The woman at the front desk said they don't close 'til eleven. You down E?"

"Sounds like a plan to me but baby I'm broke."

"I got you E. Don't you worry about nothing. G's got everything. All I want you do is to sit back, relax, and enjoy yourself. You hear me baby girl?"

"I hear you."

"Here's the room key. Why don't you run up to the room and freshen up a little and then go down to the boutique and pick up a couple of outfits and a bathing suit and meet me at the bar."

All she could do was smile but she had to admit that walk to the elevator was one of the longest of her life. A multitude of thoughts ran through her head and she only wished that she had taken the advice she'd given her good friend Leah only a few months earlier. Life had been good then—well better anyway. But with the passing of the months and Ms. Lena's death she at nineteen was feeling broken and tired. She was tired of he grueling business of men having their way with her for a few bucks and her having to be subservient to their kinky wants and demands. These men who were afraid that their wives and girlfriends would think them strange and freakish came to her to act out their fantasies and fetishes and for a few bucks she was forced to let them degrade and demean her in every conceivable way. At least as Ms. Lena's where she was being paid for her services she could half way rationalize their abnormal behavior with the fact that it wasn't many a doctor or lawyer that was being compensated as she was to endure such behavior but now she had to work twice as hard for not even a portion of the money she was making to be debased by some asshole who wouldn't dare let his wife or girlfriend that he wanted to piss on her or have her piss or shit on them. Then those that only wanted her to withstand the pain of them fucking her in the ass or being fucked in the ass while they jerked themselves off. And at nineteen she had had enough of sucking dicks and jacking a nigger off. She had had enough of sex and all of the muted and distorted ways men chose to take the emotion and love out of the act and make it a horrible aberration. And men just like G, who had a little extra to spend always believed that because they had a few extra dollars in their pockets they could do just about anything they wanted to her and get up and walk away because they had tipped her well. As Ebony reached the elevator doors she had everything she could do to just maintain her balance and not pass out. A well dressed older gentleman who saw the young lady swaying as she started to pass out grabbed her by her shoulders in an attempt to steady her and asked.

"Are you alright young lady?"

"Yeah, yeah. I'm fine. Thank you sir. I must have had a little too much to drink," she said in her best attempt to smile.

"You need help getting to your room or do you need me to call somebody?" He asked the genuine concern evident on his face.

"No, I think I'll be fine now," she said her embarrassment showing.

"Okay, ma'm," he said before waiting another minute or two before getting lost in the bevy of people in the hotel lobby.

Ebony cursed herself for making a scene and then proceeded into the elevator and made her way to the room, which was plush and must have cost G a pretty penny. Her thoughts then turned back to G as she tried to figure out his angle. She hadn't seen him in three or four years and now here he was out of the blue to her rescue on a night she certainly needed rescuing showering her with gifts and propositioning for an all expense paid night on the town like some knight from King Authur's round table coming to rescue the damsel in distress. Hell, that was only in books and fairy tales and in her nineteen years there had never once been a man to rescue her from anything. The closest thing there were to knights were the men who came to spend a few nights or months with her mother before turning around and heading for the hills when her mother informed them that she was pregnant again and the child was likely theirs. The Gs she'd met were pretty much the same. But at least they tended to be more upfront and paid before hand and left abruptly and as soon as services were rendered. And as far as she could see G was no different except that he hadn't really asked for anything and had been there when she first entered the game and now that he was back with a little cheddar was spending money like a kid with a new toy. It was a little too surreal for her and she wondered if he weren't a cop but quickly threw out after thinking of the coke he'd bestowed on her. Still, he could be undercover 5-0 just posing as an old friend. But any half ass court appointed lawyer would have the case thrown out for entrapment so that couldn't possibly be his angle and she knew his brothers and they were all drop outs who turned to petty crime and done bids so that couldn't possibly be it. And when Ebony had exhausted all the possible angles and the coke and heroin and Hennessey seemed to have all positioned themselves quite nicely in her brain she closed her eyes and fell into a deep sleep.

It couldn't have been more than a half an hour—at least it seemed like a half an hour when she felt someone shaking her lightly and calling her name.

"E baby. You okay?" Ebony slowly opened her eyes and glanced around. She'd awakened in so many different hotel rooms over the past two or three years that there was little panic in her eyes just time before she could get her bearings. Was this the Bristol, the Hamilton or Motel 6? She just hoped it wasn't the Hamilton with all its vermin. She had stayed there on numerous occasions and once awakened with bites all over her legs and stomach from bedbugs. Another time she'd awakened with lice or as they are more commonly known, crabs. But once her eyes adjusted to the light she saw that the room was not only clean but pristine with its tiny chandelier and soft colored walls. As she slowly rose from the bed she saw G sitting on the loveseat watching what appeared to be some kind of sporting event on the TV. The sound was down and she heard the smooth crooning of Kem coming from the small stereo by the bedside. Lying next to her was a woman's garment bag sporting the name of the ladies boutique she had passed downstairs in the lobby. "Go ahead baby open the bag. It's yours. I sat at the bar for about forty-five minutes waiting for you and when you didn't come down I came up to check on you and you were out. I figured you were tired so I checked the labels in your clothes and got your sizes and then I went down and tried to pick out some things I thought you'd like. How'd I'd do?"

Ebony was shocked. Looking through the garment bag she was pleasantly surprised to find that he had exquisite taste. One of the items she particularly fond of was a simple black dress to which he added a genuine pearl necklace and pearl bracelet. She'd never been real fond of pearls but with the dress she had to admit that she looked if nothing else elegant.

"Do you like the stuff? I haven't had a chance to ever really go shopping for a woman. In fact you're the first and I hope the last," he said tickled with himself. "But the sales clerk helped me out a lot. Like I hope you can help me out tomorrow when I go shopping for my moms," he said grinning from ear-to-ear.

Ebony was still in awe but managed to go over and give the young man a hug, which seemed top lease him immensely.

"You know I've waited three years for that baby. When I left North Carolina I never said anything to you but everyday that I went out there to put in work I said to myself that one day I'm going back to get my woman."

"And who would that be," Ebony teased knowing he was referring to her.

"You know damn well I'm talking about you," he said hardly smiling anymore.

"I know good and goddamn well you ain't talking about me G Rodriguez. With all those fine ass J-Lo looking women up in the Bronx I just know you ain't had your sights on me for the last three years. Don't give me that shit."

"Believe what you want but when you know what you want all you do is focus on your goal, set your sights and then pursue it until you reach your goal. I was gonna save my little speech for tomorrow over breakfast but ain't no time like the present. I want you to know that over the last two or three years I've been pretty much keeping tabs on you through Carrie and Ms. Lena."

"Stop lying. Those are my girls. They would have told me if you had called inquiring about me."

"Well, you certainly can't ask Ms. Lena but the next time you talk to Carrie ask her if she didn't get a Western Union for fifty dollars a week without fail over the last three years. I can tell you when you were arrested, what the charge was, the whole nine. Last May when you were at Club 69 and were charged with public intoxication for throwing a chair at some guy who was trying to push up on you and Ms. Lena refused to bail you out who was it that did ?," G said smiling.

"So when I heard that times had just about hit rock bottom for my girl and I had saved up enough to get married and a house and to branch out on my own I figured I'd come down here and scoop your ass up."

The nap had done wonders to clear Ebony's head and now that it was clear G had thrown her a curve and she was once again a cesspool of mixed emotions.

"And the whole time you were here you never let on to anything of this. I mean we grew up together and hung out you never let on to any of this?"

"How could I when we were sixteen you weren't just earning E. You were making a killin' and here I was this broke ass Puerto Rican papi runnnin' around tryin' to buy a dime of blow and a blunt so we could get high together. I didn't have shit to offer my girl. And you was up here makin' a thousand a night. So, I did the only thing I could do and put in plenty of work just so I could come back and be with you on an even playing field."

"And so you consider us even now." It was all a bit much to grasp and Ebony had to take a moment to sit back and laugh.

"I mean you didn't contact me once and then you just coming down here and without a word just think you're going to swoop me away. Is that it? The only reason I was out there at sixteen was because mama couldn't raise us all on the little money that she made. And you see me still out here so you should realize nothing's changed," Ebony said as the tears began to well up in her eyes.

G felt for her but had grown cold in the time he'd spent in New York. Bitch should have kept her legs closed he thought to himself. Ain't no reason for her daughter to have the responsibility of taking care of a bunch of younguns she ain't have nothing to do with being there. If the bitch would've had half a fuckin brain she wouldn't have put that shit on Ebony to begin with. His moms hadn't been the greatest either but ain't no way she would have let any of her daughters be out there in the streets selling herself to take care of some shit she'd done. Ain't no way in hell. If he had been in Ebony's shoes he would have gotten up and left and never looked back. But he wasn't E. and never would be and in a way that was one of the things that attracted him to her. Despite her mad good looks she wasn't stuck up. She was down to earth and compassionate. And despite the bitterness the streets can bestow upon you she still remained soft and humble as one could be growing up in the game.

"I hear you baby," he said gently, "but you can't always be expected to carry the weight of the world on your shoulders. All I'm asking is that you help me carry some of the burden baby. Listen, my uncle has just given me the opportunity to branch out on my own—you know open my own spot out in Nassau County. It's virgin territory and with his political connects we wouldn't have a problem with the police and he'd supply us. In turn, we'd give him ten percent of all the proceeds and he'd supply the muscle—you know—should we ever need it. And with my experience it's a piece of cake. The only thing I really need is a trustworthy lieutenant and I can think of anybody better suited than my future wife. You feel me?"

Ebony was truly flattered. Just the idea that anybody would even consider her with her storied past to be wifey material was beyond her comprehension.

"But why me G? You know I don't know anything about the dope game other than that was a shit load of blow that you gave me. And good too. Shit still got my nose burning."

G. laughed.

"Ain't much to the game baby. A month or so from now you'll have the basics down. All it is a little math and if I remember correctly you were Mr. Thomas' prize student. Math used to be your thing. We'd all be sitting in the back of the class crackin' jokes and scratchin' our heads and you'd be up at the board explainin' that shit +etter than Mr. Thomas. Now if you can do that you've conquered half the game already. The rest is just knowing and reading your clientele. There's a lot of shysty motherfuckers out there always tryna run game but it ain't no difference than the games they try to run on you now. Only difference is that dope fiends can be some of the most treacherous motherfuckers out there. When a nigga starts jonesin and needs his shit he's liable to do anything to get it. And that's why we are trying to eliminate all the street shit and just wholesale. It keeps the heat down too."

"I feel you G. But after three, close to four years in the city I know you must have built up some pretty close ties. So, why would you choose me instead of somebody already down that knows all the ins and outs of the game?"

"That's a good question E. And I'll tell you why since you asked," G said before stopping to sip his dink and hit the dope again. "That's a really good question E," he said taking his time to let the coke and Hennessey settle in. Passing the cellophane to Ebony he watched as she wrapped it up and put it down on the night table without bothering to take a hit.

"That's one of the reasons right there," G. said smiling,

"What's that?" Ebony said looking slightly bewildered.

"Cause unlike me you know when enough is enough. But it goes even deeper than that E. The niggas in New York do know the ends and outs of the game but every one of them is on the come up and I'd be hard pressed to watch both my back and my front. That's real talk. And when you trying to make some paper—I mean some real paper you ain't got time to watch both your front and your back. I want someone who wants to run the race together not someone who is more interested in being the kingpin than making the cheddar. With you as my wife and partner you'd be trying to make our life better—not yours and not mine, but ours. If you was to hold out on me you'd only be holding out on yourself and that wouldn't make no cents and no dollars. I need someone with a vested interest in us and I think that person would be you and so without any further ado I'm asking you to not only be my partner but my wife as well."

And with that said G., dug deeply into a small carry on bag and emerged with a small jewelry box. He ring inside was anything small and Ebony could only gasp, her breath all but a distant memory now as she gazed at the marquis diamond that looked to be at least three carats.

"Oh my God! No, you didn't. And to think up 'til now I thought you were just selling me a line to get me into bed but you were serious the whole time." The tears welled up in her eyes for the second time that night only this time she didn't fight to hold them back and they flowed freely down her dark cheeks.

"Dead serious and even more serious about your answer. So what's my answer?"

"Oh G. it's beautiful but will you give me a chance to think it over and talk to my mother before I give you an answer?"

"In the morning then. We'll stop by your mother's house first thing in the morning and we'll sit down and work something out so she and the kids'll be provided for."

Ebony stared at the diamond adorning her long slim finger and marveled at the brightness, the clarity and the fact that this man valued her enough to want to make her his wife.

"Let's change and go downstairs and celebrate for awhile."

"Sound good to me." Ebony agreed smiling broadly and each went into a different part of the suite and in a few minutes emerged looking like two Marc Jacobs models. Ebony in her black evening dress and pearl earrings and necklace resembled one of those Ebony magazine models we see so often with a cheetah on a leash standing by the newest make of Cadillac. Not to be outdone G. looked like he could have been Idris Elba's understudy in American Gangster. Walking hand in hand to the lounge all eyes centered on them but neither noticed so engulfed were they in the affairs of the night, which was about to change their lives. Sade oozed from the speakers as they seated themselves at a lonesome table in the very back of the lounge. Here they held hands while G. whispered all the sweet things he'd saved up to say to her in the three years since he'd been gone. This was the day he'd worked so hard for so long. Even though she'd delayed her response he was confident that she'd be his wife by the same time the next day. It was well past 3am when both decided that they were tired of passing the cellophane wrappers back and forth and sipping Hennessey.

Ebony was even more surprised when they entered the room and got comfortable, she in her new nightie, they said take me my love that G. kissed her on her cheek and eased into bed right alongside of her said goodnight and was snoring loudly within minutes. And Ebony knew right then and there what she was going to do and how she would respond the following day. She knew right then and there that if she never ever had sex again it would be one day too soon. The streets had taken their toll but Ebony tried to stay upbeat. Still, at times she loathed men for their one-dimensional sexual side that dispelled all her myths about men. There were no knights in shiny armor. There were only modern day cave men that had thrown away their clubs and replaced them with Amani suits and baseball caps. But they were the same and evolution hadn't done a damn thing to increase their brain size or capabilities. They still wielded their dicks around like a heavy crane operator dropping it wherever they saw something they could scoop up for little or no effort. She was tired of them and their careless, emotionless, don't give a fuck attitudes. And although she had neither seen G. in three years nor was completely sure of either his motives or intent he still presented more of a resemblance to those knights in shining armor than she'd seen in her short but eventful life. As good as everything seemed to Ebony she still had her reservations. This was not the first time seemed to be headed in the right direction and had taken a turn for the worse despite all her hopes and dreams. She felt a   n difference now and refused to let herself be carried away by G.'s kind words and gestures. And despite his kinds and words and gestures there was still mama. As much as she wanted to escape the hell that was Raeford, which was her life she knew that her family was the determining factor. Mama could wish her all the best and man u to the task at hand. But that would seem too much like right and when had mama ever considered anyone else but herself. Ten damn kids and nine different last names. No, all mama thought about was what appealed to her at that particular moment and it hardly ever had anything to do with her children. Mama's criteria for choosing men went a little something like this.

"Oooh that is one pretty nigga. And did u see the niggas eyes? Girl, you know I gotta get me some of that pretty nigga with the light eyes."

That's pretty much mama went about choosing her men and her next baby's daddy and nine months later there was another screaming little bastard for Ebony to feed. She didn't know why she felt such guilt in telling her mother that she wanted to move on with her life. After all her mother didn't feel any guilt about saddling her with another mouth to feed and clothe. Shit, she had been hooking for more than three years, six, sometimes seven days a week and she had yet to get pregnant. Birth control pills were free at the clinic downtown and yet every time she looked up mama was pregnant. Just wasn't any excuse for it and yet the only thing that bothered her was the fact that she had to talk to mama and get her blessing in the morning.

Ebony put her head down on the clean white Marriott pillow and glanced over at G. who was now snoring rather loudly before turning over and closing her eyes. The night went faster either she wanted or expected and she felt more fatigued than when she'd gone to bed last night. In part Ebony attributed a lot to all the alcohol and coke she'd done. But she'd had hangovers before and this was different. A cup of coffee did nothing and she knew at once that most of her angst came from the fact that she was in no way ready to face mama and the task at hand.

G. packed both her stuff and his with Ebony doing little in terms of assisting the young man who was doing his best pretending to be the dutiful husband. Attentive as he could possibly be he simply couldn't understand her sudden apathy but bore with as best he could attributing her melancholy to her just being quiet.

"You ready to go love?" G. asked.

"Guess as ready as I'll ever be. You know as much as I appreciate everything you did for me last night and as flattered as I am with your proposal I would rather say no than to disappoint mama."

G. was more than a little angry but in his short time in New York he'd learned one thing if nothing else. Things seldom worked out the way they were supposed to. A lot of New Yorkers referred t this as Murphy's Law. There was even a song that went to number one talking about this rather unique phenomenon, which states that whatever can go wrong will, wrong. It's a more or less pessimistic look at life and not one that G. embraced fully but he was well aware of the fact that it did exist. And in his business whatever could go wrong usually did and so when Ebony had second thoughts in the morning after a relatively good night G. took it all in stride beyond his years and continued on with his plan as if he hadn't heard her at all.

"Ready when you are love," he repeated.

Ebony adorned in her new black sweat suit rose slowly from the bed and grabbed the new Coach bag he'd purchased for her the previous night and made her way to the door which he held open for her. Her mind elsewhere at a place only she was aware of turned to G. and stared coldly at him before speaking.

"I thought you were going to take care of me this morning."

"In the entire time I've known you have I ever broken my word to you E.?"

"No, but sometimes people have a tendency to conveniently forget."

"Don't you ever get me mixed u with ordinary people. That I am not. In case you haven't realized that already. How many of these kids running round here my age can hold a motherfucker candle to me baby. I'm G. baby. Ain't nobody do it like me and I ain't even close to being finished. When I get done in the game, I'm gonna be a motherfucker legend. Niggas gonna be talkin' 'bout G. for years to come. And that's real talk baby. Remember those words baby. Trust!" G. said slightly angry that she had even questioned him about paying her for services yet not rendered. If anything she should be paying him he thought to himself. Ungrateful bitch he mumbled to himself as he slammed the door.

Minutes later they pulled up in front of her house.

"Let me go in and talk to mama first. I promise it won't take long but I can't promise you anything G. Just you promise me that if it doesn't go the way we planned you won't be upset with me."

"I won't be upset because I'm not letting her run roughshod over my baby. I've got this, you just wait here until get back." With that said G. sniffed what he'd poured on his thumbnail and opened the car door and walked up the walkway to the front door of the small mill house.

"Good morning Ms. Jones. Don't know if you remember me. My name is Geraldo but most people just call me G."

"Of course I remember you. You used to be sweet on my oldest. I know your mother too. Oh, what is her name? Amelia Rodriguez. Yes, I remember you G.," Ebony's mother sizing the young man up.

"So, what do I owe the pleasure of your visit G.?"

"Well, ma'm. I've been in New York for the past three years working for my uncle but I always said that when I saved enough money I was going to come back and marry Ebony."

Before he could finish Ms. Jones screamed.

"Oh, my God. I always said that that child was special. Out of all my children she's the one that has always been so blessed. But then her daddy was special too. You know he's some kind of bigwig in Raleigh. Does something with the government. I'm not sure what he does. But anyways getting back to Ebony. That is so wonderful." She said jumping up and hugging the boy warmly. "Oh my God. Oh my goodness. I really don't know what to say," the woman said her eyes welling with tears.

"I don't know what to say. Thank you G."

"That's all I wanted to say Ms. Jones. Ebony was somewhat worried that you wouldn't bless her matrimony and sanction our marriage."

"And why wouldn't I? I'd have to be one selfish mother if I did want to see my daughter get ahead in life. These streets ain't got shit to offer her but a slow death and I done seen to many of my friends and family die as a result of them. I don't want to see my daughter be eaten up by them. Hell, if you can offer her a better life then I'm all for it. I only want the best for my child. And if you promise to provide that for Ebony what can I say? You have my blessings G."

"Thank you Mrs. Jones. That I can do. I promise you. I have no doubts that I can do that but Ebony has her druthers about leaving you with the kids."

"Oh, hell Ebony's always been a worrier. Kids and me will be fine. We always have been and we always will be," she laughed. "We're Black folks and Black folks are survivors," she said laughing again though her laugh and her attempts at levity didn't have quite the sincerity as it had before. G. who had become somewhat of a master of watching people's body language got up from the loveseat he had been sitting in and approached the older woman.

"Mrs. Jones I know wanting the best for Ebony is what you want for your daughter but I also know that what she brings to your home will be sorely missed and I also know that raising a family is rough in this day and age and we will try to pick up where she left off."

Mrs. Jones' pride forced held her to speak up but G. cut her short.

"Pride is a wonderful thing and I wish a lot more people had it in my line of work but pride don't pay bills. So, instead of saying anything just take this," he said holding out his hand. "This is just a little something that should tide you over until we get back to the city and get on track."

A teary eyed Mrs. Jones held out her hand and took the money without counting it and stuffed the bills into her bra and thanked G.

"Where's Ebony?"

"She's outside in the car. I asked her to wait there until I spoke with you Mrs. Jones. I thought it only right that I asked you for her hand in marriage and your blessing."

"You have my blessing son. Now would you be so kind as to get my daughter."

G. walked outside a grin a mile wide etched across his face.

"Ebony sweetheart your mother would like to see you."

Ebony still somewhat nervous allowed G. to open the door and then grabbed his outstretched hand and allowed him to escort her to the curb.

"How did it go baby?" she asked. "Did she take it well?"

"What's my name baby? I could sell ice in the Arctic and rice to a China man. What do you mean did it go well? By the time I was finished she had three or four of your little sisters lined up to marry off as well. What do you mean did it go well?" G. laughed.

"Then she said yes?"

"Of course baby. Gave her a little something to tide her over too until we get settled in too."

"Oh, G." Ebony said smiling as she hugged him and tried to kiss him at the same time. "We're really going to do this ain't we?"

"Damn sure are baby. We going to do the damn thang. And we gonna do it like it ain't never been done before," He said laughing as he grabbed her hand pulling her up the walkway.

She was surprised at how well her mother so readily accepted the idea of her leaving and both shed tears as Ebony hugged and kissed her brothers and sisters goodbye. It was touching to say the least and even G. had to walk away and regain his composure.

In the car Ebony broke down completely and G. had to pull to console her.

"It's not like you won't ever see them again E. We can drive down every couple of months to check on them and we can send your moms a little something every month to make sure she's okay."

"I know but it's just that I've never been away for them any length of time."

"And you don't have to be now. The first thing you need to do is get your driver's license and you can shoot back down here when you get a mind to."

Ebony continued to let the tears flow freely when she caught G. smiling sheepishly through tearful eyes.

"What the hell are laughing at?"

"Wasn't laughing was just smiling at a thought I had."

"And what thought is that?"

"The thought that you're ballin' your eyes out over being homesick and we've only gone two blocks."

They both laughed. The rest of the trip was somewhat calm as the two friends reminisced over days past and dreamed of a life together. So far what G. had pleasantly surprised Ebony had become since leaving Raeford. He'd gone from a timid young boy to a strong and confident young man but she had no idea just how successful he'd become until she saw New York and how he certainly wasn't one of the bottom feeders just trying to scrape out a meager existence. No G. had a loft down on the lower eastside that rivaled anything she had ever seen. Not only was it spacious with two huge bedrooms. But the den that sat off from the bedroom was a large as the four bedroom home her mother owned in Raeford. Not only was it spacious but it was tastefully directed with African American art dispersed freely but tastefully. Ebony had never seen anything quite like it but refrained from oohing and ahhing too much in her attempts to be coy and not to be so in awe and not to show her ignorance or lack of culture. However, it soon became obvious as G. showed her the landmarks and other noteworthy sights. When she did show her naïveté he only laughed and gave bear hugs to his little princess. He paid no mind to the fact that she was for all essential purposes a little country girl who knew little more than the Bottoms where she'd lived a cloistered life amongst the poor of rural North Carolina. He had been the same when he'd first arrived until his uncle and others schooled him on the New York state of mind and although it had been slow going at first he'd eventually picked up the subtle nuances of what made a New Yorker special. And so would Ebony. At night when they returned home after a day of sightseeing and familiarizing her with the streets and subway system he'd take her home where the real education began. G. educated her on both levels of his business taking her from the young hoppers who stood look out to the junkies and crackheads and all the games that they'd run. He then showed her middle management where the street playas who considered themselves ballas would roll thru asking for half keys or keys to put out on the streets and be back in a day or two to reup. These were the ones you had to watch closely because these were the ones that were on the way up and in money making Manhatta there was little else that mattered other than the cheddar and they'd just as soon shoot you on the come up as give you some dap. Opportunists is what G. called them but Ebony had problems differentiating them from everyone else in New York. To her everyone here seemed to cutthroat on the edge. She remembered G. showing her The Garden where the Knicks played when a car had pulled up on 33rd alongside the Garden and damn near hit a pedestrian who was crossing the street and was well within his rights. The pedestrian though was like most New Yorkers, short tempered, in a hurry, and not disposed to anyone entering his space pulled out what appeared to be a thirty-eight cursed the driver out before continuing on his way. No, New Yorkerd weren't to be fucked with and G. made this point clear and dope boys on their way to becoming one of the rich and famous were even more dangerous. Most of them had something to prove and aspirations which no man or woman was going to come between. The Columbians and Dominicans who were the main suppliers were less dangerous but with the weight they moved and money involved you didn't want to be a day late or a dollar short or you'd be found belly up in the Jersey swamps. Ebony took it all in and watched G. as he worked from several of his uncle's bodegas in Spanish Harlem and the Bronx. She took in everything and at night it became little more than a question and answer session. Her knowledge growing Ebony felt that she was finally ready to try and handle her own business. That night she approached G.

"Baby it's been close to three months and you've let me handle some business and told me that I did a good job. I think I'm ready for my own spot. I mean what more do I need to know?"

G. smiled and did his best not to seem patronizing but this was no small matter. Here she was the woman he was growing more in love with each passing day willing to put herself on the front lines. There was no doubt she had the heart but there were so many variables, so many threats and despite her savvy and heart this wasn't Raeford. These niggas here looked for any weakness they felt they could exploit and when they found it in many cases it was lights out. G. knew this and as adept and knowledgeable as he was when it came to the dope game there were days, and more than a few, when he worried for his own life. It was even more difficult to throw his future wife out to the lions.

"I know you're ready E. but I'm just not all that comfortable leaving you out there on your own yet. Just be patient baby. You'll be there before you know it."

"If you didn't feel about me the way you do and if I were anybody else I'd be out there stacking papers already. Tell the truth G."

"You probably right E. But you ain't just anybody else. You're my woman. And most of these motherfuckers out here know that so they not just gonna come after you. They gonna come after you sideways. They know you're the closest person to me so they ain't comin' just to rob you."

"Ah, c'mon G. What they gonna do. I been to the pistol range and even you said I could defend myself a lot better than a lot of your members of your own crew. So, what's to be afraid of? If you're running one spot and I'm running another that's twice the loot. C'mon G. think about it?"

"Trust me beautiful. That's all I have been doing is thinking about it. I hear everything you said and the money would double but we have to be smart about this. I know there's no guarantee but I want to be sure that you're insulated from all harm. You understand what I'm saying?"

"And while you're trying to insulate me from harm we're losing money."

It was obvious that G. was angry now. It was the first time she had actually seen him angry and it frightened her a bit.

"Baby, are you happy?"

A little taken back by the question Ebony hesitated before answering.

"Of course I'm happy G. I'm happier than I've ever been in my life. . You know that. I don't even know why you're asking."

"And do you have everything you want?"

"Pretty much but what's the point?"

"The point is and please help me to understand why someone that's happy and has everything hey could possibly want is so anxious to throw herself in harms way."

Ebony dropped her head in embarrassment.

"I make a living risking my life everyday selling fools this poison and I want to ask them the same thing but they're customers and I truly believe that every man has the freedom to choose how he lives and how he wants to die but for the life of me I can't understand someone that's giving the blessing of life wanting to chance it on a fifteen minute high. Just don't make no fucking sense to me."

"I hear whatcha saying baby but I been hustlin' ever since I can remember and now you want me to just sit back and chill while you shower me with shit. I mean I'm not sayin' that I don't appreciate it but I ain't never been a kept woman. That just ain't me I need to be active and doing something. I can't just sit idle G."

He smiled now. His parents had told him the same thing when he was thinking about moving to New York. There words though true and on point hadn't done any good then and his words were falling on deaf ears now.

"Why don't you think about taking a class or two at CCNY or something. I'm gonna need someone to handle the books baby."

"Hire an accountant G. I don't want to be counting the money. I want to be making it. I ain't even tryin' to spend it. I just want to make it," Ebony said almost pleading now.

G. understood. Bowing his head his anger subsided, he took a few minutes in an attempt to regain his composure before speaking. There was no smile now. His approach solemn he addressed her.

"I understand you E. You like the hustle. I know brothers out here that are just like you. The money is the motivator and they define themselves as men by the amount of men they clock each day. Trust me and you know I love you but that's a dangerous game to play."

"What's so dangerous about that sweetie. If you make four or five grand a day and I make the same it just means that I'm keein' pace and holdin' my own with my man. I can't see what's so wrong with that."

"There's a lot wrong with that E." G said his anger rising again. "First of all, there's a problem with chasing the almighty dollar and the problem is that it's fleeting but if you continually chase money it will turn on you and consume you either with greed or cause you to make mistakes that can be costly. When I first got here my uncle sat me down and told me a story. He told me how two men started off at the same point and decided to race across country from New York to California. One gut bought a hot rod that was all souped up and could do somewhere around a hundred fifty to a hundred sixty miles per hour. The other guy bought a regular family sedan. Anyway the one got in his hot rod and peeled out from the gate driving a hundred and fifty. The other guy did the speed limit and when he got tired he rested at the local motel while the other decided he wasn't going to sleep at all. Well, the guy in the hot rod that was racing to get there was pulled over several times and placed behind bars for everything from reckless driving to speeding. While the other saved gas by doing the speed limit, and was well rested for each leg of his long journey. The first guy lost so much time and money by speeding, driving recklessly, and spending so many nights in the pokey that a mile or so from the finish line who pulls up beside him but my man in the sedan. The guy in the hot rod is so outdone that he stomps on the gas but he's so tired and spent that he misses the up coming curve and goes headlong over the embankment and not only loses the race but loses his life as well. You see E. life is nothing but a race. It's a marathon and you have to show some patience if you want to finish in the winners' circle. You can't just go out there running recklessly. Real talk."

Ebony fixed G. and herself a glass of Zinfadel and turned on the smooth sounds of Will Downing as G. spoke. Handing him the glass and lighting a cigarette for him she looked into his eyes which were glassy and red from lack of sleep.

"I get your point baby and I really hope you don't see me as that guy rushing headlong into disaster. I've never been reckless. I guess I'm just a little anxious is all."

"A bit of angst is good baby. But make sure you know how hot shit is before you're will to throw your hand in the fire. And I ain't never lied to you the shit is hot out there. You'll see. Tomorrow we ain't gonna have the comfort of working out the bodegas. No, tomorrow you're gonna see the game for what it really is. We got a lil spot up on 145th and 8th. The spot is good for twenty to thirty g's a week but in the last two to three weeks it ain't been bringin' in but about six or seven g's. There's definitely something wrong. The brother that handles it has been a consistent earner for my uncle for years but the word on the street is that he's either usin' or tryin' to make moves on his own. So, you and I and a couple of my boys are going to work it for the next couple of days and see if it's the corner or if my man really is shaky. This is where the shit really gets gully and grimy. There's a fifty fifty some ol' wild shit is gonna jump off and truth be told I really don't want you no where's around but it's all about educating you to the game. My uncle and I had words over this shit. He thinks I'm coddling you too much and thinks a bit like you that you need to be out there in the mix and get your feet wet whereas I think your ass should be as far away from this as I can get you."

"Oh G. you worry too much. I can handle myself. I'll be fine."

"I sure hope so. I don't treally think you know how I feel for you. I've always had mad love for you. And if something should happen when we're so close to being husband and wife and maybe starting a family of our own I think I'd die."

"Trust me baby, I'll be fine," she said taking him in her arms and kissing him lightly, then gently on his mouth.

"Can I ask you about something though that's totally different from what we've been talking about?"

"Sure baby, you know you can ask me anything. Fire away."

"Well, I've been here for close to four months and not once have you touched me or tried to make to me. Yet, I know you love me and have been around enough men to sense that you want me in that way. So, why haven't you even tried to make love to me?" Ebony asked as much out of need as curiosity.

The smile returned to G.'s face as easily as it had left.

"How long has it been E.?"

"Four months and I'm starting to feel it. You know that first night we were together in Raeford I was so happy that there was finally a man that liked me for something other than sex. I mean I knew yhere was or at least I had to believe there was in order for me to keep my faith in men alive and then lo and behold your ass shows up and I'm like—thank you Jesus, I knew there was a God—but then days and weeks and then months go by and you still haven't approached me or even given me the slightest hint that you want me. I mean I know you do but you haven't tried to take me. I guess I just don't get it. You've done everything you can to make sure I'm happy but you act like you don't want me. Is it because I was a prostitute?"

G. burst out laughing as he took Ebony in his arms and kissed her hungrily. Not to know what to think and wondering if he was laughing at her she pushed him away angrily.

"The fuck are you laughing act. That's it ain't it? You figger you're too good to stick your dick in a prostitute but you're kissin' a prostitute. You're kissin' the same mouth that sucked somebody elses dick."

G.'s first reaction was to haul off and smack the taste out of her mouth but his better judgment held him back. He could feel himself trembling out of anger and clenched his fist in an attempt to hold back the rage that raced inside of his tightly built frame. He could remember the day that Black Mike had come to school with the news that she was prostituting herself. Mike and he had been boys for as long as he could remember but he had come as close to killing Black Mike as he ever had to any man and the two had never spoken again. Even when he came to the realization that the rumors were true G. had a hard time accepting the fact that another man had been up in his woman and tucked the reality in the dark recesses of his very fertile brain. Now here she was bringing it to the forefront and all he could envision was her gasping for her last breath as he choked the living shit out of her for having the gall to diminish his queen to a common street whore. And then like a revelation it all came to him as he turned from her. The last thing he wanted to see was this woman, his woman, as a common dick-sucking whore.

Grabbing his jacket, and his shades G. turned abruptly and headed for the door. He hadn't made his rounds in some time and he realized that he hadn't really been on top of his game since Ebony arrived in New York, He also knew that he wasn't in any kind of mood to deal with silly niggas that weren't handlin' theirs. He seldom let his emotions get the best of him when it came to business. After all, business was after all simoly business but the idea that his woman had actually wrapped her gorgeous lips around some other man's penis fucked with him. Other woman could do it but not his. G. started the black Mercedes SUV up and bent down to grab the bottle of Hennesey under the seat checked the cd player and took a long swallow from the bottle before tossing the empty bottle out onto the grassy curb. Pulling onto a side street he picked up his tiny cell from the console and called his second lieutenant and enforcer.

"What's up Blackman?"

"Same ol same ol. What's up my brother?"

"Not a damn thang. Just makin' the rounds. Wanna ride?"

"Sure. You holdin' anything?"

"I got a little somethin' somethin'."

"Where you at?"

"On 7th in front of the Drew Hill Projects. Where you at?

"Just left the lounge. 'Bout to get on the West Side Highway. I should be there in about five minutes."

"Damn I didn't know you was that close, Give me time to get my clothes on and I'll be down."

"My bad. You with Cherelle? I ain't mean to interrupt yo thang man. I'm good. You go ahead and lay up. I got this."

"Is you crazy nigga. When my boy G. say you wanna ride I know my pockets gonna be tight. No nigga you wait. I'm on my way down as you speak."

G. laughed.

"You's a crazy nigga Tone. Ain't no way I'd leave a fine ass like Cherelle to come out here to fuck wit' some knucklehead niggas."

"That's 'cause I'm tryin' to get where you already is nigga. Besides you know how we do. Money over bitches baby."

Both men laughed.

Tone was waiting at the curb when G. pulled up.

"Oh shit the nigga got the Mercedes tonight. What's up G.? What's up with the Mercedes?"

"Ain't nothin' just got to keep these niggas guessin'. Never let 'em clock you. Anytime a nigga get comfortable, think he know your pattern you got to change it up on 'em. You know keep it new. Gotta keep them niggas off guard."

"I feel you," Tone said unwrapping a cellophane wrapper and handing it to G.

"What's up with that shit?"

"Dunno. Some shit D-Nice gave me. Said I should taste it and hook up with him later. Said he gotta connect wit' weight and the best prices. Told me to test the product. Claims it's some straight up killa."

"You taste it?"

"Nah baby. Only thing I been tastin' is Cherelle's sweet ass. You know she ain't down wit' no drugs so I'm a straight up choir boy around her."

"Is it that good?"

"G. the bitch almost had me ask her to marry me tonight. That's why I can't be going up there on the regular. I mean she don't cook, clean, nothin'. She just throw me a lil taste of that good good every now and then and my shit be on swoll. It's motherfuckin' scary."

G. laughed.

"Let me tell you Blackman. There are days when I get up and my dick will tell me to cancel everything and go see Cherelle. And I be like yo Dick you know you my boy and everything but we need to stop by TeeTee's. I say you know the rent's due and TeeTee say she got the rent this month and all I gotta do is stop and hit it one time and we straight for the month and that one eyed fuck will look straight up at and me and say 'is we going to Cherelle's or not?' I look that bastard straight in the eye and say fuck no we going to TeeTee's and take care of the rent. And you know what that motherfucker asked me? He say you can go to TeeTee's if you want nigga but let me ask you something before you get there. And I says what nigga? What you wanna ask me? And he say you can go to TeeTee's but have you ever had erectile dysfunction before 'cause I swears I's saving my shit for Cherelle."

G. doubled up over the steering wheel in laughter.

"You dumb Tone. You my nigga but I swear you crazy as all hell."

"Real talk though G. You ever love a bitch and in your heart you know she ain't right for you? I mean you love her to death but like your values just ain't the same. Like you see something so clear and plain and she can't see shit and like the whole time you tryin' to move forward she's sabotagin' your shit and all you doin' is treadin' water or makin lateral movement but ain't no forward progress? That's Cherelle. She killin' me G."

"On the real son, she can only do what you allow her to do. A man ain't gonna let no bitch take him somewhere he don't wanna go."

"You right. Hate to do it but I'm a have to cut her off. The pussy's is the bomb but she's about to drive me crazy. How's your shorty treating you?"

"The same as yours. 'Bout to drive me crazy. She thinks she's ready to open up her own spot but I don't really want her mixed up in this shit."

"I hear you G. Shit, I'm gonna tell you something that I don't even tell my woman but if I had to do it over again I'll be damned if I would ever choose this shit. I mean the cheddar we make is fabulous. I don't know too many doctors and lawyers clocking the dough we be hauling in but I get so tired of waking up and looking over my shoulder wondering if the police are gonna lock my ass up or shoot me. And when I look over the other shoulder there's some dope fiend intent on tryin' to rob my ass and shoot me for some shit. You know I don't tell many people this But I finished high school and got accepted in Cornell. Now I wish I had went. These streets ain't nothing but poison and I live every day like it's my last and that ain't no way to live if you ask me. I used to think it was but I've made it, had nice whips, beautiful women, the best dope and where I am now none of that shit means much."

"I hear you Tone. But let me ask you this. If you wasn't in the game what would you be doing?"

"Barbecues and baseball games," Tone chuckled. "I'm telling you G. I'd have a slave—you know a nine to five and a wife I'd do my damnest to keep barefoot and pregnant. I'd get me a small house out on the Island where I'd just chill. Might even take up golf and fishing."

"You kidding?"

"Dead serious. If you wasn't my boy and I didn't have to look out for your country ass I'd be out of the game already. You know that while all the rest of them niggas is out there tryin' to be King of New York and sippin' Christal and chasing hos the kid be investing in his own 401K. This shit don't last long. Ain't no future in it. The key is to know when to walk away cause eventually your number comes up."

"You ain't never lied," G. commented as he pulled the Benz over in front of a crowded corner on a 145th and 8th. Both men surveyed the scene before getting out.

"You strapped?"

"Always. But you know these weak niggas ain't bout shit. Jay got these boys locked down anyway. He a good brother. Always comes correct and handles his blocks. He one of those niggas that is sho nuff in line for a promotion."

"You right but ain't no tellin' when one of these fools wants to be the new sheriif in town. You strapped?"

"Even when I sleep," Both men laughed.

"That's a damn shame G. You know this ain't no way for a nigga to live." The two men crossed the busy avenue together, Tone stood six four a mountain of muscle while G. stood only a couple of inches shorter and could have passed for a weight lifter or trainer. The two posed a threat to most but even more to those who worked for them and word of their previous dealings with those who had crossed them was almost legend now. Still, the two moved with caution.

"I know it ain't none of my business G. but try to keep your shorty out of the game as long as possible. These streets ain't got no love for nobody."

"You right. I just wish I could get her to understand that. My uncle wants us to take over Trey's spot for the rest of the week."

"Is that nigga still coming up short."

"Appears so," G. commented nonchalantly.

"You think he's skimming off the top or using?"

"Coming up too short to just be using. He's definitely skimming off the top. Word is that he's about to start up his own spot."

"Stupid ass. Greed is a motherfucker ain't it," Tone said lighting up a Newport.

"Anyway, I'm bringin' E. out so she can get a taste. She might change her mind after a couple of days uptown."

"I didn't change my mind and neither did you. Matter of fact you were out there bright and early your second day. I remember me and the fellas fell out over that shit. You had your little white dress shirt on and black pants. We didn't know if you were going to the prom or going to work at McDonalds. You was one country nigga," Tone said recollecting.

"Fuck you Tone," G. said smiling.

The two men had known each other since G. was just a small boy and his mom would let him spend summers with his uncle. Uncle Ray though married had never had children of his own and adopted both boys and reared them as if they were his own. Ray welcomed the company of the two and from the moment they met they were inseperable. Tone had even gone to North Carolina to visit G. once or twice and when his mother died Ray adopted him although there were no official papers stating this.

Being in the city and living with Uncle Ray he'd gotten into the game a couple of years ahead of G. but had always shunned the spotlight and seemed satisfied to be the muscle of the family. Tone was the only person G. trusted and referred to the rest as snakes. Now here up on 145th and 8th the two were once again the faces. Respected by all, the two approached the spot and were greeted warmly by everyone. A large Black man with tattoos covering his entire body quickly approached the two men. "What up G., Tone?" There was no love in his eyes only the steely cold that the penitentiary instills in a man after too many stints there.

"What up Jay. How we doing tonight?"

"Makin' it brotha. Just makin' it."

"You wanna drop with me now or you wanna wait til' tomorrow?"

"I gotta few things out on consignment and a few people still ain't paid up. You know they're good customers but it's early still. They'll be in before the nights over. But if you need it I can run to the house and get it for you."

"Nah, Jay. Tomorrow's fine. Any problems?"

"Nothing I can't take care of but tell Ray I'm not going to need anything for a minute. Maybe three or four days."

"Why, what's up?"

"Nothing. Just some folks 'round here who want to try my kindness. They want to get stupid over some product but you know that's all part of the game. It's to be expected. Every now and then you have to make a statement and hurt somebody and let them know you ain't to be fucked with. And so I've got to put some work in tomorrow and I guess by the time the whole thing blows over it's going to be hot as hell on the block for the next two or three days."

"I understand Jay but do me a favor don't do anything until I make the pick up. I don't want to get pulled on a routine stop when they looking for you or one of your crew."

"Okay baby boy. Listen though as soon as this thing is done I'm outta here. Maybe even before. I've got an airtight alibi. Gong to stay with my sister over in Jersey for a couple of days cause I'm a two time loser and ain't lookin' to pick up no third strike so try and make the pickup early in the morning if you can."

"I'll be over here at around nine on my way to work."

"Sounds like a plan G." Jay said before pulling him close in an embrace before turning around to serve two waiting customers.

"Love you bro," G. said in parting.

"Back atcha my nigga," Jay said not even bothering to turn around.

G. looked around. It was easy to spot Tone who stood a head taller than anyone in the crowd.

"Let's bounce my brother."

"We good?"

"Tell you in the car."

The two men crossed the street just as they came quietly and aware of everything around them.

Once inside the car both relaxed somewhat, the threat all but gone.

"So what's up G. Everything good?"

"I guess as good as can be expected. You know Jay's straight. I'm gonna put in a word with Ray and see if we can get him something a little more low key. He's a good brother but being a two-time loser he don't need to be out there all high profile and shit. You know he's a two time loser?"

"I feel you there but I don't know what else the brother can do. He's a soldier and muscle first that's primarily why unc has him running shit. He's got the roughest blocks out here and there ain't never no problem. He's the reason for that. He's fair and everybody knows that but they also know if they fuck with him there will be hell to pay. You know I fear no man but Lord knows I wouldn't want to cross hairs with Jay."

"He's scary. Said he killed a man and maimed another in the same fight and came out without a scratch."

"I heard that too and don't too many motherfuckers fuck with him but somebody did which is why you ain't going near there tomorrow. Said he don't want no reup for a few days. He said he's got to put some work in tomorrow and is shutting it down for a few days."

"Don't know who crossed him but I wouldn't want to be that motherfucker. That nigga don't know it now but he gonna find out that he bit off more than he can chew and that's word. So, I want you to stay clear. Whatever Jays got planned ain't good and he told me that shit is gonna be hot there for a few days so I want you to stay clear."

"You know me G. The only trouble I'm looking for is between the legs of some big legged woman."

"You always did like 'em big didn't you," G. laughed.

"Love 'em big. Feel like I'm getting' my money's worth."

"You ain't lyin' about that. That one shorty you had…What was her name?"

"You talkin' 'bout Tanya?" Tone grinned.

"Yeah Tanya. Hell, I believe you got your moneys worth and somebody else's too," G. laughed. "Shit, I remember seeing her coming around the corner of Lenox and 155th one day and I drove around the corner five minutes later and her ass was still on 154th."

Both men bent over in laughter and G. had to swerve to miss a black Volkswagen heading his way.

"You crazy as hell man. Tanya did have a big ass though. I used to sit her on top with her ass in my face and just be amazed. That shit was like the eighth wonder of the world to me. Sometimes I used to sit and marvel at it. To this day I ain't see nothing comparable."

"And your ass probably won't. You know that shit was deformed."

"Deformed hell. That girl had some good pussy."

"I'll never know." G. replied pulling over onto the Grand Concourse.

"How you wanna handle this shit G. You know as well as I do that the nigga gonna come

up short."

"I ain't gonna do nothin'. I don't want no drama. All I'm gonna do is ask him to drop

the money, count it and report whatever he gives me to Uncle Ray. End of story."

"Sounds like a plan to me. Then we shoot over to the South Bronx and then back to Cherelle's sweet ass and I'm what four or five hundred dollars richer.

"Tone adjusted the steel plated Glock in his waistband before getting out and followed G. by a few paces. Hey both knew that Trey had his crew staggered along the street and these kids had no sense. Most of them would shoot their own daddies for a buck fifty and not shed a tear. Aware of this they wouldn't make it easy if there was gunplay and almost always stood apart from each other so as not to get hit by the same bullet or spray from automatic wepon.

"What up Trey?" There was no love as there had been with Jay and G. always made it a point to keep it strictly business when dealing with Trey. G. had long ago had run ins with the young man when they were vying to come up in the game and the rivalry had hardly dissipated.

"What up G.?"

"Ain't nothin'. How are sales?"

"The same ol' same ol'. It's slow."

"So you don't need to reup?"

"I'm not sayin' that. Just sayin' it's a little slow right now but it's early. I expect it to pick up in a little while."

"Alright. I'm going to leave you with a hundred dubs. That with what you have left should take you through the night. You know Uncle Ray has me and Tone and the crew up here for the rest of the week so ain't no need for you and your boys to show up tomorrow."

"What the fuck is that?" Trey said raising his voice and triggering his boys. A couple moved in to see what the problem was.

"Uncle Ray just wants to shore the block up. He's not understanding why sales are falling. But I mean look at it as a vacation. Take your crew and go down to Miami or the Bahamas for a couple of days. Have a good time. We'll hold it down 'til you get back."

Trey ignored G. His thoughts going back to the days when Ray had chosen G. and Tone over him when it came to naming a lieutenant. He had never lked having G. as his superior and he didn't like it now.

"Motherfucker you don't tell me what I need to do."

His crew sensing a problem circled the two men.

"A problem boss."

"Chill nigga. Maybe you don't know who this is. This is the nigga that pays all of you."

The man stepped back a bit.

"Right now he's also the man who's trying to lay us all off."

G. watched the crowd of young men whisper among themselves as Tone stood quietly under the awning of the storefront next door watching apprehensively. He'd been through similar scenarios and although this was his function, his job, he neither enjoyed it nor looked forward to the impending drama. Still, he stood back, a curious onlooker waiting for the scene to play out before providing muscle if needed.

"What up with that nigga?" A large burly nigga looking like a cross between Heavy D and Biggie said.

Seeing what Trey was trying to initiate G. didn't back down.

"Don't believe I know you brother. My name's G. And here's the deal. I'm the supplier. I supply Trey with enough dope to keep the fiends fed and all of you should be eatin' and be fat but the money keeps coming up short and I know you niggas is out here workin' hard but the supplier ain't be paid. And me and my partners no this is one of the hottest spots in the city." G. paused to light a cigarette and let his words sink in a bit before continuing. "At first we thought someone was using but anyone using that much would be pushing up daisies so it's obvious to me and my investors that someone is skimming off the top."

"What you tryna say nigga," Trey said reaching into his waistband.

"Wouldn't do that if I were you Trey. That would be a fatal mistake," came a voice from the back of the crowd. Everyone turned and looked at the man they had let go unnoticed. Tone stood, a sawed off shotgun pointed in Trey's direction. G. flicked the ashes ignoring Trey and continued.

"Our job is to make that paper and there's enough paper out here in these streets where would we should all be eating, getting paid, and living large." Then just to add the coup de tat he selected the worst looking nigga in the crew and addressed him personally. "Nigga," the young boy turned around to see who G. was addressing. Yeah nigga. I'm talkin' to you. What you take home last week?"

"Me?"

"No nigga not me. You. I asked you what kind of paper you took home last week?"

"I don't know. Somewhere between two fifty and three hundred."

G. looked at Tone and both men laughed.

"Nigga you might as well be working for Wendy's."

"Ngga when we was out here slingin' and that was what G.—six, seven years ago niggas would laugh at you if you told them you weren't makin' a 'g' a night. Am I lying G. Somebody got y'all asses hoodwinked. But I'll tell you what? Me and G. will be out here tomorrow and any of you who want to make some real money will be here too. We'll show you what real money is. Not like punkass Trey who ain't nothing but a little thievin' punk who's ripping both of us off. The man wants us to shore up the block and give Trey the benefit of the doubt but I'm tellin' you now my brother if I ever see you in the neighborhood I'm a personally cap your ass. You understand?" Trey didn't say a word as Tone walked up to him sawed off shoddy still pointed at his stomach and took the gun from Trey's waistband.

"Now git."

"You ain't heard the last from me nigga."

"I know. You gonna come correct before you go anywhere homepiss," G. said holding out his hand.

"Gotta run to the house."

"We'll take you there." Tone replied. "Ain't nobody trustin' yo snake ass."

"Any you fellas wanna make some real money be here at twelve tomorrow." G. said looking back at the small posse still standing there.

The two men escorted Trey to the car one on each side. Minutes later they pulled up in front of Trey's apartment building got out and went upstairs. The small apartment was sparsely decorated but well kept. Once inside G. made himself comfortable, pouring himself a glass of cognac.

"Nigga may be a snake but he got good taste in liquor." G. said.

Tone kept a close eye on Trey following him into the bedroom. The loudmouthed Trey was now quiet. He'd come up with both men, started out with both in the game and was well aware of what happened to niggas that skimmed Uncle Ray. The accusation had been made and that was all that was needed. All Uncle Ray had to do was think that someone was ripping him off and he'd send Tone to settle the score. But Tone had the authority to make that call in Uncle Ray's absence and more often than not Tone would eliminate the problem instead of checking with Ray and having to make a return trip. Usually that meant lights out fro the guilty party involved and Trey who had been on an outing or two with G. and Tone years earlier certainly knew that.

"So what we gonna do G." Tone asked still keeping an eye on the young man now kneeling and opening the tiny wall safe behind the headboard of his bed.

"I'm a have me another glass of this Grand Marnier and then we gotta make this last stop over in Bed Stuy and call it a night. I may do that in the morning. It's always less drama when you go in the morning. Ain't gotta worry about the fiends being up that early. But Black is always correct anyway."

"I'm not talkin' about Black. I'm talkin' about this nigga. Should we do him tonight? We could get it over with now and won't have to worry about this low-life motherfucker tryna thieve and backstab nobody else."

"Do you what you feel Tone."

Trey was still fumbling with the safe. His hands shook and no matter what he did he couldn't steady himself.

"Baby, just could the money and let me go. I promise you won't hear or see me again. Just say the word Tone and I promise you Tone I'm ghost"

Tone ignored Trey's words and moved closer to the man kneeling.

"Hurry the fuck up and the money best be correct nigga."

"It's correct Tone plus I got a little I been saving up for a rainy day. It's yours too if you just let me get a pass this time Tone. Tell him to let me get a pass this time G. for old times sake."

"For old times sake," G. laughed. "I didn't like your ass tthen and I still don't like your monkey ass. I might be the wrong person to ask."

"C'mon G. you know it wasn't nothing personal. It was jus business."

"Still is. That's why my boy guy gotta handle his business so he don't have to worry about a slimy ass sneakin' in the cut and tryin' to get some payback."

Trey opened the tiny safe and took out six stacks of paper and separated them into two stacks.

"What the fuck you doin' nigga?"

"I gotta have something to live on—you know—to try and get a fresh start."

"To live on?" Tone laughed. "And what the fuck makes you think you're gonna live?" Tone said drinking the rest of G.'s cognac.

G. who was now standing at Tone's side and over Trey snatched the money from Trey's hand.

"Damn Tone there must be close to two hundred grand here. No wonder Uncle Ray been coming up short and them niggas ain't been getting' paid."

"Shoot that fool Tone. G. said with little or no compassion."

"Oh God no," Trey yelled the tears pouring from both eyes.

"Rock a bye baby," Tone said pointing the gun at Trey's head before squeezing the trigger. The sound of the hammer as it clicked was all that could be heard as Trey fell to the floor. A large stain ran down the leg of Trey's pants.

"Oh shit, this nigga done pissed himself," Tone said laughing.

"Git up nigga and pack yo shit up up. And if you're ass is still here in the morning I'll shoot you myself. Ya heard me?"

Trey nodded weakly but did not even attempt to get up.

"Oh yeah and thanks for the cognac." G. said as he grabbed the bottle off the living room table and followed Tone down the stairs of the tenement and out to the street.

"You know I should have offed that nigga G. That sneaky motherfucker is the kinda nigga that will spend the next ten years plottin'."

"Nah you did the right thing Tone considerin' we have to post up up here for the next few and we don't want to draw no heat."

"I guess you right. I just don't trust him."

"Neither do I but I don't think he'll be around anytime soon after he came that close to meeting his maker tonight. He should be counting his blessings for the next week or two."

"How long you think he been skimmin' off the top?"

"For sometime now to have two hundred grand stashed away but I don't wanna talk about that loser anymore. You wanna run over to Bed Stuy real quick or you think we should wait til tomorrow."

"Tomorrow sounds good. Besides Ray should be pretty pleased with this pick up alone." "Okay, then we're you headed my brother?"

"Guess you can drop me where you picked me up G. Hold on and let me see if she's still awake." Tone said taking his cell and dialing Cherell's number/

"No answer. I guess she's asleep. She did say she had to get up for work in the morning."

"I asked you if you wanted to ride when we first started out and you told me money over bitches so don't start crying now. Besides with the pickup we made tonight Uncle Ray gonna pay you enough to go up to Hunts Point after work tomorrow and buy you a ho. And you know how you like them hos up there under the bridge?" G. laughed recalling the time when they had been kids and Tone had gotten his first pice of pussy from one of the prostitutes up at Hunts Point.

"I'll never forget that da you came home happier than a faggot in Boy's Town cause you had finally broke your cherry and gotten a piece. The next day you were screaming like a little bitch talkin' bout how the bitch had given you the clap. One minute you was cryin' in pain and the next minute you was sayin' how you wasoin' to murder the bitch so me and Uncle Ray went with you down to the clinic where they gave you a shot. I believe that was Wednesday and Friday when we got paid and I asked you where you was going you said that the shit was so good you were going back to get you some more" Both men fell out.

"Take me over to TeeTees. Ain't seen her in a minute.'

G. did as ordered and minutes later he found himself down in the East Village.

"Pick you at about ten. Be ready nigga."

"Always ready. You be safe my brother."

Tone slammed the car door and G. soon found himself back out in traffic. After three years he still hadn't gotten use to the fact that the city, his city like him never slept. Moments later G. pulled up in front of his building and looked left and right before exiting the vehicle. By now it had all but become a formality. A formality that his life depended on and so he went through the ritual before unloading the night's haul and grasping the handle of his pearl handled thirty eight he exited the car and made his way to his building.

Opening the door to his apartment he was pleasantly surprised to find Ebony's long legs escaping the blanket under which she slept peacefully. Locking the door he turned around and focused his gaze on Ebony and had to admit that she was one beautiful Black woman. Damn! New York was the capital when it came to beautiful women but this poor little girl from the Bottoms of North Carolina could rival the best of them. G. closed the door gently so as not to wake her and stood there mesmerized and marveling at her beauty. Feeling his eyes on her Ebony slowly turned and acknowledged the man standing over her.

"G. I'm so sorry for saying all those terrible things. It's just that I'm used to be so active, you know always working and rushing from this place to that and having the responsibility for taking care of the kids so this is all new to me. This being a kept woman and I guess whereas a lot of women would love to be in that role. I really have a problem with it.

If my man is out there hustling to make it then I want to be right out there with him. Do you understand what I'm saying? It ain't so much about making a dollar as it is about me being able to contribute. Do you feel me?"

G. smiled proudly understanding completely. He'd felt the same way when he'd first arrived. But his uncle had been cautious, taking him under his thumb and walking him through every phase of the game. And despite her anxiousness he was adamant about bringing her along in the same fashion despite her impassioned pleas and talk of her being ready. After all, it had been more than three years and he still didn't feel he was ready. In fact the more he immersed himself in the game the less he felt he knew.

"Not even worried about that little scrap and that's not to say I wasn't listening to you E. It's just that you're my heart and my soul and this is a dangerous business so I'm going to do everything I can to make sure that you're safe and out of harm's way. I have the responsibility to you and me. Don't know whether you understand but these streets are a little bit different than what you're used to. But it's a lot easier to see than for me to tell you. Tone and I are taking over a spot uptown where this nigga was skimmin' off the top so you'll get a first hand chance to see what life's really like out there in the streets and if you can handle that then we'll set you up in your own spot within the next couple of weeks. Ecstatic with the news, Ebony jumped up from the couch and hugged G.

"Oh, baby I will make you so proud of me."

"I'm already proud. Just remember that there is no amount of money that can replace you in my heart. Just remember that," G. said pouring himself a glass of Henessey. He'd need it with the day that was fast approaching.

They made love that night and though neither said a word it was the first time that either had felt quite that way. For the first both knew what it was to be in love.

The following day came with a rush. Ebony was up early making coffee and puttering around the kitchen. Dressed in a black Coogi sweat suit she grabbed the pot of Folgers put it on a tray with a single red rose, two slices of toast with a smattering of butter and made her way to the master bedroom where G. was still sleeping soundly.

"Wake up sleepy head," Ebony said kissing G. lightly on his forehead.

"What time is it baby?"

"Eleven thirty."

"Oh my God! Why didn't you wake me up?" G. said jumping out of bed. "E. can you do me a favor and run down to the corner cleaners and tell MR. Sing that I need my navy blue Nike sweat suit."

"Damn baby! A good morning would have been nice. Or even a thank you baby for fixing breakfast."

G. laughed.

"Sorry sweetie," he muttered grabbing a slice of toast on his way to the shower. "Good morning," he said kissing on the cheek before slapping her on the ass. "Now could you please run down and ask Mr. Sing to give you my navy blue Nike sweat suit and tell him I'll pay him tonight when I get home from work."

"I heard you the first time. Oh, and Tone called you twice."

"What did he say?"

"You know he doesn't talk to me. He just asked to talk to you and I told him you'd call him when you woke up."

"Hand me my phone please bay."

"Okay! What's it going to be? The clothes from the cleaners or the phone?"

"I'm sorry bay. Go ahead and grab my clothes and call me on my cell so I can see where I put the damn thing."

"You got it your highness. Will there be anything else?"

"No I'm good."

Two minutes later the phone rang. G. thanked Ebony, hung up and immediately called his boy.

"Overslept Tone. What up?"

"Nothing man. Ray called and wanted to know where we were. I told him I was waiting on you."

"Thanks Tone. Can always rely on you to cover for me. I'll be there in a few. Where you at? You still at TeeTee's?"

"Naw man. I'm uptown at the Drew Hill Projects. Met Cherelle up here on her lunch break for a little of that afternoon delight."

"Man the way you working your boy he gonna be ready for early retirement in a few."

"Nah nigga just keepin' my johnson in shape. I'm waiting for them to make bonin' an Olympic event so I can go for the gold. You know I'm a shoo-in if they do that," Tone laughed.

"Don't know if you a shoo-in for that but you sho nuff for Bellevue's Psychiatric Ward. That's for damn sure. Anyway, let me jump in the shower. Be outside. I'll pick you up in fifteen or twenty minutes. Be ready."

"Yo, G. did you talk to your girl about this shit."

"Yeah but it fell on deaf ears."

"So she's coming?"

"Yeah she'll be there."

"I was gong to talk to her but I didn't want to seem out of line."

"You wouldn't have been but sometimes experience is the best teacher."

"Problem is experience can be deadly."

"Truer words ain't never been spoken."

"See you in a few."

"Peace."

Few words were spoken as Ebony and G. headed uptown. Rush hour traffic had long since subsided so the trip uptown only took minutes.

"What's up Tone?" muttered Ebony a smile on her face. The two had become almost as close as the two men and were constantly at each other's throats laughing and teasing each other. G. never interfered or got involved and was genuinely grateful that the two got along so well and so it was nothing when Tone picked up the mantle and tried to talk Ebony out of the drug game.

"Yeah, I hear you Tone but where else is a woman gonna be able to contribute and make a contribution to the household equal to her husband's workin' a fuckin' nine to five and that's even if I were able to get a job. Hell, with my record ain't nobody gonna give me no job."

"Why would you wanna work anyway? This nigga makes enough for four or five niggas twice his age. And trust me he didn't go all the way down to North Carolina to pimp you on these streets. The only thing out here in these streets is death and hard times. I seen it. And believe me you don't know or want parts of either one."

"I ain't worried about either one of them or anything else with you and G. around," she laughed.

"With us around? Nigga wanted to shoot G. last night. Hell, girl we be dodgin' death everyday."

G. shot Tone a sideway glance that said that he said a bit too much but Tone ignored him. No, G. she needs to know that this game we playin' ain't like the Barbie and Ken she used to. This here game is only about one thing baby and that's ducats, dough and dollars and who got 'em and what a nigga's willing to do to get his and yours too. Ain't no rules to this game and these fools will cap your ass for ten dollars."

They were pulling up at Trey's old spot. A crowd of young boys was already milling around eager to get started.

Tone exited a small duffel bag under his arm and Ebony closely by his side.

"You two go ahead. I'm going to run up to Uncle Ray's and give him what I got."

"No problem I'll set things up here," Tone said.

G. was back in an hour or so and though business was slow for lunchtime he had every one in place and pumping product fairly well. Most of the dope fiends eyed the trio of G., Ebony and Tone suspiciously at first but when they saw the rest of Trey's crew conducting business as usual they proceeded throwing caution to the wind. It was the same with the police who circled several times wondering whether or not they should harass the newcomers. Still, most of the attention came from the statuesque Ebony who mingled with the crew and did her fair share of slinging.

"How you doing baby," G. asked at around six thirty. "You tired?"

"No, I'm good."

"I hope so because in another hour or so it's really going to pick up."

"I'm fine baby. Go ahead handle your business."

"You are my business baby. I love you," G. said walking away.

Tone was doing his thing. Standing back, keeping the peace and checking out the sistas that happened to pass by Tone was in his element. Everyone now and then a sista would pass by on her way from work and he'd strike up a conversation but his attention never left Ebony as she dealt with the ease and composure of a veteran street player.

"Nah nigga a dub is twenty not fifteen," she said with cool aplomb. "Come back when you can come correct or don't come at all. This is a business baby not a charity."

Both Tone and G. smiled as the young dope fiend eased away from Ebony then over to G. who figured to be an easier touch.

"Brother man I'm a few bucks short. Why don't don't you let me get a dub for fifteen?"

"Sorry my man. You heard what the lady told you. Ain't givin' up no shorts today. Come back when you have the whole twenty and then we'll talk."

The man looked at G. then at Tone.

"Damn man where's Trey? Trey knows I'm good for it. The nigga would front me all the time."

"That's why Trey ain't out here no more Tone interrupted. "Now move on. You're holdin' up business."

The man glanced at Tone's rather imposing figure and eased on down the street muttering to himself. Tone turned to G. and made the comment.

"You girl's going to be alright G. She handles herself well to be a rookie. Is she strapped?"

"I gave her a little twenty two. Enough to keep the dogs off of her but not enough to really do me any damage."

"You gotta give it to her. She's handlin' business."

G. smiled with pride.

"That she is."

The day went on with only a minor skirmish here or there and the money rolled in. G. and Tone were both in there element and around one o'clock in the morning G. whispered to Tone that they were somewhere between twelve and thirteen thou wg=hich was a good take for a Thursday night and gave real promise for the weekend. And being that the first of the month was tomorrow and Friday he expected no less than a hundred large for the weekend.

"That should do us around thirty g's for the weekend," Tone said a little concerned. It had always been a two way split but now that Ebony was in the picture he wondered if it were going to be a three way split. He'd never had to worry about it before but now that he thought about it he wasn't sure why he hadn't brought it up earlier.

"How's your girl figger in."

"I got her. I'll just take it out of my cut."

"Wh don"t you just let Ray figger her in and that way we'll all get even shares and it'll come outta his cut. That's the least he can do since we're taking him from somewhere around twenty g's to upwards of a hundred g's. You kow what I'm sayin'?"

"You right. I'll run it by him after tonight. I don't see why he wouldn't. Good lookin' out Tone."

"Not a problem."

The night ended with no major problems. Oh, there was a minor skirmish here and there. A crack head tried to switch some soap with a vial of crack and was caught dragged into an alley and his fingers promptly broken but aside from that and the fact that so many customers were upset that there were no shorts being accepted by this new regime it was a fairly quiet night.

The trio in charge paid everyone and all seemed fairly happy with the new management and the raises they received. Uncle Ray was negotiating a new deal with the precinct commander to insure his boys' safety form harassment and the world once again looked promising for Ebony, G. and Tone.

When it was all over G. breathed a sigh of relief and thanked Allah for having made it through another night.

"Anybody wanna stop for a drink?"

"Hell yeah!" Ebony and Tone said in unison before bursting out in laughter.

"I can understand how doing that shit every night would wear on your nerves," Ebony commented to no one and everyone at the same time. G. shot a look at Tone and both smiled and dropped their heads.

"And believe it or not tonight was a good night." Tone commented.

"I told you that experience was sometimes the best teacher," G. said commenting to Tone.

After a couple of drinks the trio headed back to the East Village.

There was no lovemaking on this night and as soon as Ebony's head hit the pillow she was asleep. The rest of the weekend went pretty much in the same manner and each night Ebony came home a little more disenchanted than the night before.

"This shit is whole lot more stressful than I thought. If it ain't the fuckin' fiends tryin' to get over it's these low life bottom feeders trying to push up 'cause they got a few dollars in their pockets."

G. heard her but said little. In only a couple of days she'd come to see that it wasn't all the glamour and glitz that she'd envisioned.

"You ready to leave it alone," G. asked.

"Yeah, I guess I am. In the whole time I was in the street I never imagined people could be so fuckin' grimy and gully. Nigga told me he would lick my pussy and let me pee on him if I wanted him too. And all the nigga wanted was a dime. Ain't that some shit?"

G.'s expression didn't change. He knew it was just a matter of time before she'd see. Still, he never wanted Ebony to see the seamier side of life and talked to her 'til he was blue in the face so she wouldn't have to encounter what he already knew but she wasn't hearing him at the time. He even had Tone talk to her. After all, they knew. But no, she had to experience it first hand. Now she had had a taste of it and he only hoped it wouldn't change her as it had him. He'd become bitter, cold and calloused for such a young man and there was no going back or erasing the fact that the streets had taken him from an innocent child to a man with little hope and faith in mankind. In the beginning money had become his God, his savior, but that was not sustaining and not enough now. He'd even gone home in attempts to rekindle his spirit and his soul and sought out the one good thing he could remember from a childhood void of love and now she was caught up in the mix he had sought so hard to have her avoid.

"So you're not going out with us tomorrow?"

"No, I agreed to work the week and I'm going to finish the week out but soon as the week is up I'm going to enroll in CCNY and get my degree. I think I would do a lot better trying to teach some kids about avoiding the pitfalls that I fell into and feel a lot better about myself as a person than simply making money. Besides my soon to be husband makes more than enough money to sustain us. I may even minor in business and open a small business when I get tired of teaching. You know I used to do pretty good in school."

"Who you telling? I used to sit in back of you in Ms. Robinson's class just so I could cheat off of you. That's the only reason I passed her class," he laughed.

"Oh, no you didn't," Ebony yelled. "And here I was thinking that I was half way cute and you were sitting next to me because you liked me."

"Well, that too but mostly because I could cheat off you," he replied laughing again. Ebony took the pillow and slapped him upside the head.

They made love for the second time that night and G. was surprised that it was even better than the first night. Life couldn't be better. He was making money and putting it away for the day they could buy a simple home and just sit back and relax in each other's company. They had already decided on downsizing to a more modest one-bedroom apartment in Jersey just past the Palisades. And in a year or so he planned on opening a bodega or two in Paterson, which had a sizeable Hispanic community, and no Hispanic grocery. They planned the marriage for the following week and would invite only Tone and Uncle Ray. G. suggested her inviting her family but she was against that saying that they'd have to charter a bus to bring mommy and all her brothers and sisters. Besides she was content to keep it small and intimate. Ebony's words warmed G.'s soul and he was glad to have chosen a woman with her guile and common sense. He loved her deeply and had never loved a woman as he did Ebony. He'd often told himself that there was no future in the game and never planned to be involved any longer than it took for him to legitimate himself. In the four years or so his uncle had not stressed anything more than the fact that the only pension for a drug dealer came with prison or death. And the only smart dealer is the one that leaves the game alone as soon as he makes enough to do something else. G. had heeded his words. He didn't know how many dealers he'd seen have to give it all for a ten or twenty year bid upstate. No matter how smooth they were their number eventually came up. And by no means had he considered himself any differently than those he'd seen go before him. He knew it was just a matter of time before his number would come up. And that's where Ebony came in. She was his stabilizing force. She was his ace in the hole, the person he would ride off into the sunset with one rainy afternoon and he couldn't think of any better time than now. He'd finish the week off with his true love by his side, ask Tone if he would like to join them as a partner and the three of them o start over somewhere far from the maddening crowd. But until then it was business as usual. And so after a glass of rose he kissed Ebony goodnight and headed off to bed.

"Daddy ain't gonna give his lil' girl no good-good tonight?"

"Daddy's a little tired tonight but you know I got you. I'm gonna give you all you want on that sandy white beach in Jamaica next weekend," he said smiling and kissing her on her forehead again.

Ebony poked her lips out.

G. laughed.

"You used to do that when you get a wrong answer back in school. Didn't see that all that often though. You was spoiled then too." He said closing he bedroom door behind him.

Ebony put her glass down and went and sat on the couch pulling her knees up to her chin and pouted. She'd committed the act thousands of times but had never been in love before and was weak for this man. Now she felt like she'd been smacked hard by his rejection. Still, she felt a warm glow inside. If nothing else she knew that her man loved her as she'd never been loved before. The other thing she knew was that she loved him like she had never loved anyone else in her life.

The sun burst through the sheer white curtains like it had been invited. G. rolled over and moaned in agony.

"What's wrong baby?" Ebony whispered.

"Nothing just not looking forward to another day of the same ol' same ol'. Wish I could call in sick."

"Ain't no sick days when you're self employed," Ebony replied kissing him.

"Who you telling?" G. grunted.

Ebony grabbed her robe and walked into the kitchen, grabbed the can of Folgers and measured out five healthy spoonfuls and after finding the coffee filters poured the coffee in all the while humming Sade.

"I ain't never seen anyone that's always cheerful," G. said grabbing her around her waist and hugging her tightly.

"What's not to be cheerful about? The good Lord blessed me again by giving me another day. There's a lot of people that didn't have the good fortune to wake up this morning."

"I guess you're right," G. said only half hearing her.

"No I'm not just right. I'm blessed."

G. smiled. He too had to admit he was blessed. He finally had Ebony in his life.

The rest of the day went according to plan although G.'s mind was speeding on fast forward. He was already on the sandy beaches of Montego Bay. He could remember his mother telling him when he was still in grade school to live one day at a time because life was fleeting and all those days he wanted so badly to skip so he could get to the next one could never be reversed. Still, he was tired and just ready for this phase of his life to be over. Several times during the course of the day Tone and Ebony stopped to ask him where he was and what was on his mind.

The night came early and there was little change. Business was off the hook and the combination of payday and the first of the month had Tone wondering if there had ever been a better day.

"Think we can head in a little early tonight G. We don't have much more to sell and I've already been uptown four times to reup. We can leave what's left with the fellas and let them divvy the shit up amongst themselves. Be a bonus for them. They done sold their asses off tonight. They deserve it."

Before G. could answer the sound of automatic fire they all knew so well interrupted the now quiet corner.

"What the fuck?" Tone yelled pushing G. down and pulling out his glock as a dark sedan rolled by spraying everyone. Tone returned fire hitting the driver's side several times. G. was now firing in unison but the driver and shooter obviously unscathed made a sharp U-turn and headed right for the crowd of people. Tone and G. scrambled for cover as they had done so many times before. Tone found the doorway of an abandoned tenement while G. made it to an abandoned alley narrowly missing the now swerving car. The driver obviously hit drove into the tenement a few feet from where Tone stood. The shooter had obviously been hit too as there was no fire coming from the car. Tone and G. approached the car cautiously. The driver was dead slumped across the steering wheel. The two men heard groans coming from the back seat. With a nod from Tone G. swung the back door open. A bloody figure lay on the floor begging for help.

"Oh shit G. Do you see who the fuck is riding around here playing cowboy?"

"Don't tell me it's that nigga Trey?"

"I told you I should have wasted this nigga last night. But your compassionate ass wanted to give him another chance. You can't ever trust a snake."

G. was visibly shaken. He knew Tone was right. The end of the week couldn't come soon enough. And then his thoughts turned to Ebony. She had been right by his side when the shooting had first started but in the melee he hadn't seen her. Panic in his eyes he turned to Tone.

"You seen Ebony?"

"Last I saw she was standing right next to you. If this don't convince that she don't n parts of this ol' crazy shit nothing will," Tone said still staring at Trey who was writhing in pain. "Whatcha want me to do with this piece of shit?"

"Hold on T. I'll be right back."

There were bodies everywhere. The street was littered with people. Dealers, crying out for help, innocent people on their way home from work that would never see home again and amidst them was Ebony smiling and staring up into the vacant blue sky.

Solo

He'd been hit many times before and he'd been hit by a lot bigger men but this kid could really pack a wallop. He smiled at the young boxer moving to his right to let him know he hadn't been hurt but Lord knows the kid had rocked him. Another shot like that and he would have been out on his feet. The sting of the punch was still there and the stars were only now starting to clear. Damn!

The old man had said this kid was on the come up but the way he hit, Chaz wasn't sure if he was coming up or if he was already there.

Dancing to his right he smiled trying to pretend that the stinging jabs followed by that overhand right hadn't had an affect but it did little to dissuade the kid who was now more like a raging bull than the prospect he was supposed to have been. Still, Chaz knew that all his ring years and wars in and out of the ring was the one thing that he had over the kid. The old man called it ring savvy and experience but right now Chaz called it survival. Moving smoothly out of range Chaz threw a stinging jab of his own and moved away.

"That's it baby. Stick and move. Stick and move. That's all you have to do. Show him who's champ baby," Chaz heard his corner man yell out.

Ol' Mike had been in his corner since the beginning, somewhere around eleven or twelve years now. Chaz couldn't remember but he knew the old man had always been there from the first time he'd picked up a glove at around eleven until he turned pro at seventeen. Through it all he'd won six Golden Gloves Championships and was now middleweight champ of the world although he didn't know how long he could he could retain it.

Back in the day he'd been at the top of his game and was enjoying all the glory and luster that came along with it but over the years he'd somehow grown tired and lost his love of the sport. Now here he was in the ring before a packed house with some kid who'd probably been playing marbles when he was on his way to his first Golden Gloves Championship. He almost wished there was some seniors tour like they had in golf now as he watched the Young Turk circle the ring in his best efforts to cut off the ring and pin him to the ropes where he could inflict some more damage.

It wasn't that Chaz was old. He was just old for a boxer. Sure, he still had the Mikee snap and pop to his punches that he'd had when he was eighteen but the wear and tear of being hit too many times had taken their toll. And much as he hated to admit it he'd lost a step or two. And now with the Kid bearing down on him throwing punches from every angle conceivable he knew that his days were numbered. Chaz slipped the overhand right ducked and threw two straight rights to the body. The kid felt the straight right hands and flinched from the crisp, hard body shots. Another uppercut from the crouch to the kid's solar plexus left him gasping for air and Chaz knowing that he had his man in trouble followed with an uppercut to the jaw that left the man dazed and confused. It was obvious the kid was shook and Chaz recognizing the confusion in the kid's eyes moved in for the kill. The kid was in a foreign land and was pawing for the ropes to keep himself upright but it was all for naught as Chaz closed in reigning thunderous left hooks and uppercuts from every angle. The young man helpless now reached for the ropes before that thunderous right caught him right behind the ear and left him lurching and grasping for ropes that weren't there. Seconds later he fell flat on his face as the referee waved Chaz to the neutral corner.

"Good job baby."

"And the winner and still champ. Mr. Chaz Martinez."

Chaz looked wearily out over the crowd to see if he could see his wife but Ramia had a way of disappearing if the fight got too intense or if she had any premonition of her man being hurt.

Oftentimes she wouldn't make it through the first round and he could count the times when she'd made it through an entire fight on one hand and still have fingers left over. No, she usually made her exit long before the fight was over. He was 32-0 going into this fight with twenty seven of those wins coming by way of knockout but it hardly mattered the outcome. As soon as he got hit she'd leave. He didn't know how many times she'd begged him to get out of the game and as much as he loved her he just couldn't. It wasn't that he didn't love her. She meant the world to him in a time when people got married one day and divorced the next and he had to admit that there's was different. But getting out of the fight game, well, that was just beyond his comprehension. That's not to say he hadn't given it considerable thought. He had and even more recently. But even though nowadays he was in constant pain and was beginning to have trouble gathering his thoughts and his knees hurt constantly what else could he do?

Boxing had bought them a couple of acres and a fine home on the outskirts of the city and had enabled him to provide the best of everything for his wife but after fourteen years of boxing he had little to show for it other than those few things he could readily put his hands on. He had taken on this match on short notice for no other reason than his mortgage payment and the car note were due and he'd promised himself that this time he would put everything away except those two payments but in reality he knew that the time was quickly approaching for him to find some other way to make a living. And that would certainly make Ramia happy.

How many times had he had this Mikee conversation? But rubbing his jaw and still feeling the sting of where the kid had tagged him with that straight right he was more than sure it was time to throw in the towel.

"How you feel champ?" The old man asked as he rubbed his shoulders awaiting the official decision.

"I feel good." He said as he jogged in place.

"You looked good champ. You know the promoters are talking about you on the undercard of the Chaves-Marquez bout coming up on HBO. And you know what that means."

The man couldn't have envisioned the thoughts in Chaz's head as he continued.

"They're talking maybe two, no more than three months at the latest. They're just waiting for Marquez to sign. So, you know what that means."

Chaz smiled.

"Boy, I thought that would bring more than a smile. Isn't that what we've worked all this time for?"

"Sounds great Mike," Chaz grunted. His thoughts were cloudy. Yeah, the old man was right. This is what he'd been waiting for his whole career and now that that day he'd dreamed about his whole career had finally arrived he wasn't sure that that's what he really wanted anymore.

He'd been shook more in his last few bouts than he'd been hit in his whole career and if it was one thing he knew and had to agree with Ramia on that was the fact that boxing was a dangerous game and no matter how good the money was or how loud the applause there came a time when you had to be smart enough to call it a day despite the payday and the cheers. Still, he wasn't in this by himself and as badly as he wanted it he believed the old man may have wanted it even more. He'd taken a special interest in Chaz when he was no more than eleven or twelve and raised him as though he were his own son.

The old man had been a boxer once and had come within a fight of a championship belt when a torn rotator cuff ended his career. He'd taken the loss and chalked it all up to God wanting him to focus his efforts elsewhere and that elsewhere became young wayward boys like Chaz.

Teaching him all he knew about the game of boxing the old man brought Chaz up through the ranks helping him to stay the course when other boys in the neighborhood were getting in trouble, going to jail, getting shot for senseless things and well just because they didn't have anyone taking an interest in them.

When Chaz won his first Golden Glove Championship it was almost as if the old man had won the belt himself and Chaz was never happier than to be able to present the belt to the old man. When he'd won the world championship it had been the Mikee. And Chaz knew the old man wanted nothing more than to be looked at as the corner man and the brains that'd been responsible for taking his boy to a guest spot on HBO where everyone would see and finally be forced to pay homage to the trainer who had molded a champion.

Not only that but for the first time in who knows when it would allow him a chance to fix up the gym he loved so much. He might even be able to buy some new equipment and attract the kind of fighters that would keep his name in lights.

Knowing this Chaz didn't even consider telling Mike about his plans to retire.

"I figure we take a couple of weeks off before we start training for the next bout, champ. Then we hit the gym like there's no tomorrow 'cause this HBO thing is the gateway to everything. Once you fight on live television and you're a household name you can pretty much name your price then you won't be forced to fight just anybody and everybody. You can pretty much pick and choose who you fight and pretty much pick those fighters that fit your style not like this kid you fought today. He had you in trouble for a minute there didn't he?"

The referee raised Chaz's hand and announced the official decision and the crowd cheered loudly.

"Yeah, the kid was strong as a bull. Hit me with a couple of shots that had me seeing stars but he was young and didn't know how to finish. He's going to be a pretty good fighter in a year or two. Hope I'm long retired before he gets it all together," Chaz said smiling and still holding his chin.

"Didn't know the kid was that good? Watched some film on it but it must have been old. He sure didn't look like the kid in the tapes. He really snuck in under the radar."

"Gonna have to get you a new radar detector," Chaz said still holding his chin. "I'm thinking he may have broken my jaw."

"Go, take a shower and we'll have the doc take a look at it."

Chaz went into the locker room and ran into Billy Devlin preparing for his fight.

"How did it go Chaz?"

"I won. KO'd him in the fifth but he tagged me a few good ones. I think he broke my jaw."

"You fought the kid?"

"Yeah."

"Boy kicks like a mule don't he? I fought him a couple of months ago. Lost a split decision to him. His people asked mine if I wanted a rematch and I said hell no," Billy laughed. "I ain't never been hit that hard in my life. Made me rethink my whole career," Billy laughed. "He's gonna be something in a couple of years."

"I just told Mike the same thing. Kid had me seeing stars in the first round. I said let me get this fool out of here before he gets upset," Chaz laughed.

"Well, I'm happy for you man. They tell me they gettin' ready to put you on the big stage."

"That's what they say?"

"Did you tell Ramia yet?"

"Nah, I ain't had a chance to yet."

"I don't envy you there Blackman."

"When that boy hit me I thought about everything Ramia told me and was hell bent on retiring right up 'til Mike told me that I had a shot on HBO. I'm telling you when he hit me with that overhand right I was done. When the fight was over my only thoughts was how I was going to break the news to the old man but he seemed so damn happy to tell me about the HBO spot that I didn't have the heart to say anything. So, I accepted the deal."

"I hear ya."

"But you know in all the years I've been in the game and all the money I've made I ain't got two nickels to rub together."

"You ain't alone my brotha."

"But I'm tired man. So, no matter what happens after this next fight I'm done. Win or lose it's a wrap. I'm just hoping the purse is large enough to retire on."

"I feel ya. Gain a few more pounds. Move up to the heavies and you wouldn't have to worry about shit. That's where the real money is."

"You right but if a light heavy could pack a punch the way that kid did today I don't know if I want to fuck with the heavies," Chaz laughed.

"Devlin. You're up." The short balding white man shouted.

"Alright, Billy. Good luck, man."

"Thanks Chaz. See you in the gym."

Billy and Mike touched hands.

"Good luck baby."

"Thanks pops."

The old man immediately turned his attention to Chaz.

"You're not working Billy's corner?"

"Not with my star in pain. Besides Billy's got this. He ain't fightin' nobody but that ol' washed boxer from over Dunbar's gym. What's his name? You know the boy. You fought him a couple of months ago, knocked him out in the first round."

"Oh, you're talking about Ali."

"Yeah, that's the boy."

"Billy should have no problem with him. That's an easy W."

The older man ignored the younger.

"You ready to go Chaz. Gonna drop by doc's house and then run you to the house. "

It had been this way for as Chaz could remember and he liked the fact that the old man had taken a special interest in him. Minutes later they pulled up in front of the doctor's house and knocked.

"Hey Mike, Chaz good to see you. Heard you had a fight tonight. How'd you do? I was trying to get there but the missus had some charity fundraiser she saw a need to drag me to."

"He knocked him out in the fourth. You should have seen it doc. It was a thing of beauty. Chaz hit him with a textbook left hook. It was clean. Looked like the boy started crumbling when he saw it coming."

"Is that right? Wish I could have seen it. Was the guy any good?"

"Chaz said he was the hardest hitter he's ever faced. That's why where here at this hour. Thinks he broke his jaw."

"Well, come on in and let me take a look," the doctor said grabbing Chaz by the arm and pulling him in the house.

Once in, he lifted Chaz's head and tilted it from left to right before making Chaz open and close his mouth several times.

"Doesn't look to be broken and there's little or no swelling but it's hard to tell from just a glance. What I need you to do is get a good night's rest and meet me at the hospital at nine in the morning. I'll take a few x-rays and see if anything's out of place. Could be a hairline fracture and the only way I can see anything that small is with an x-ray. "

"You hear the doc Chaz."

Chaz nodded. He shook the doctor's hand and headed for the car followed by the older man. He heard the old man muttering something but his mind was a thousand miles away. He was thinking about the conversation with his wife a couple of hours earlier. He'd promised Ramia that this was his last fight and he'd never lied to her in their eleven years of marriage. Well, that was up until now and the thought of telling her that he'd accepted one last fight bothered him to no end. He considered all the ways he could tell her but nothing he came up with would sit well with her. And every block closer to home he felt his stomach twist up just the same way it did before he left the dressing room before a major fight. Chaz felt the sweat beading up on his bald dome and he wound the window down to get some air. His stomach tightened even more as he stuck his head out the window as he began heaving.

"You okay Chaz?"

"Yeah, Mike."

"You usually do this before a fight not afterwards."

"No, the real fight is just getting ready to start."

Mike glanced over at the young man puzzled.

"I promised Ramia that this was my last fight and now I've signed on for one more."

"She ain't going to be none too happy with that you know?"

"Who you telling? I ain't never lied to her before and that's what she's going to think but I ain't got no choice pops. I took this fight tonight on short notice because I've got bills coming out the ass and I ain't got a pot to piss in or a window to throw it out of and now just when the biggest payday of my career comes along and I've got a chance to finally get straight I can't just let it go."

"You ain't signed shit yet Chaz."

"You're right pops but what choice do I have. I've waited all my life for a chance to hit the big time and to finally get paid and when the time comes I have to go through this bullshit."

"Ramia's a good woman Chaz. She ain't like the rest of these two bit ho's running round here. So, if you want to let this go I understand."

"And what would I do for money then? You know she enjoys all the perks that come with being good at what I do but she doesn't understand that ain't nothin' free."

"Just explain it to her the same way you explained it to me. She's a reasonable woman. I'm sure she'd understand especially when you explain the financial ramifications of taking this fight."

"Money doesn't have a damn thing to do with it Mike. Ramia was just as happy when we were up in that little one room flat where the heat only worked in the summertime and the air worked in the winter. All she sees is all the boxers like Ali that fought one fight too many and can barely talk."

"And she's right. Boxing is a risky game and more often than not they come out maimed or worse. More than a few even wind up dead. She's absolutely right about that. The occupational hazards are higher in boxing than in most jobs. All she wants is her husband. The money don't mean shit if you're six feet under."

"I know. You're right but this is a chance of a lifetime. We both know that Mike. And I know she's right Mike but this is something I just have to do."

"Then man up boy and go tell her. If she loves you and I know she does she'll be angry but I can't recall a time that Ramia has ever turned her back on you. It may be hard to swallow at first but she'll be right there in your corner when it's all over."

As the car pulled up to the house Chaz had a renewed sense of strength. His jaw still hurt but he now had the courage to go in and tell Ramia his decision.

Entering he was surprised to find his wife of eleven years nowhere to be found. Throwing his gym bag on the love seat at the bottom of the stairs Chaz made his way slowly up the long winding staircase and down the hall to the master bedroom only to find Ramia standing there in a sheer white nightgown. Still slim and curvaceous she hadn't changed much from the size six in the eleven years they'd been married. Standing there she excited him as much as she had when they'd first met.

"Hey baby."

The tiny young lady moved gracefully towards him wrapping her arms around his neck pulling him to her and kissing him gently on the lips. He grimaced at her touch. Noticing she stepped back.

"What's wrong baby? Are you hurt?"

"No, baby I'm okay. I won you know."

"I don't think that's what I asked," she said her face showing her concern. "Are you hurt Chaz?"

"I said no, Ramia," he said, his disgust now showing clearly in his tone."

"I don't know why you're getting upset with me honey. I'm just glad it's finally over. And you can't be upset with your wife for being concerned over the welfare of her husband. What kind of wife would I be if I didn't give a damn," she said turning and picking up a couple of glasses of Dom Perignon. "This is in celebration of a wonderful career and new beginnings."

Chaz took the glass and put it down on the nightstand.

"Ramia, I think it's time we had a talk."

"Oh, goodness. I don't think I like the sound of this. Can't we talk in the morning? I've waited three months while you were in training and went along with that silly ass superstition that sex saps a boxers energy and stamina. I sacrificed because you asked me to and now that it's over you want to talk. What don't you get silly? I love my husband and won't be put off another minute. Do you have any idea how I feel tonight, or how much I want you?"

Chaz smiled.

"I can imagine."

"Aside from the day we were married this may be the happiest day in my life. No longer do I have to worry about some brute trying to take my baby's head off or the crazy schedules that dictates when a husband and wife can love each other. For the first time in our marriage we can live like normal people. You don't know how long I've waited for this day."

"Sit down Ramia."

From the tone of his voice Ramia could tell Chaz was more than a little annoyed but what had she said? Only hours ago he was in total agreement and now this. What the hell could have possibly happened during the interim?

"You didn't even ask me if I won and am still champ?"

Ramia smiled coyly.

"Win or lose you will always be my champ. Besides I already know you KO'd him in the fourth."

"And that should have been it but there were some executives from HBO looking for a prime time boxer to add to the undercard of the Chavez-Marquez bout and after seeing me knock this young buck out they talked to Mike and well I accepted the bout."

"You did what?" Ramia screamed. "But I thought we agreed that this was your last bout. Less than two hours ago right here in this bedroom you gave me your word that win or lose this was your last fight. You gave me your word!"

"I know baby but I was looking at the fact that the mortgage and car note are both due and what do we have in the savings. What?! About seventy dollars?! We're broke baby!"

"And? It's not the first time we've been broke but we've always found a way to make it. We've always gotten by."

"True but what would you propose I do to pay the bills after this month?"

"You do what most normal people do. You get a job."

"C'mon Ramia. What the hell kinda job am I gonna get that's gonna pay the mortgage on this house let alone three car notes. I don't even have a GED."

"You don't need one baby. You can go and do trade shows. Whether you recognize it or not you're a celebrity. You can do speaking engagements for civic agencies. You can go back to school and speak to kids about the pitfalls of dropping out of school. You can run a gym and train young boys in the art of boxing. It's not like you don't have options readily available to you baby. The only thing you don't have is the confidence to get out there and take the bull by the horns and that's only because you've been in the ring too damn long and you think that's your only option when in truth the whole world is at your fingertips."

"It's just that not easy Ramia."

"You're wrong Chaz. It is that easy. The only thing difficult about the whole thing is change. But don't feel bad. Most people are afraid of change. After doing something for so long it's extremely hard to

change but there is no doubt in my mind that you can do it. I've seen you where you were damn well out for the count and you drew from some inner strength and picked yourself up and went on to win the fight."

"That's boxing baby. We're talking about fighting. That's something I know and done all my life."

"Ain't no difference. Life ain't nothin' but one long continuous fight. You should feel right at home baby."

"I hear you bay. But do you realize that with the payday from this one fight we'll be set for life."

"Do you know how many times I've heard that over the years Chaz?"

"I know baby but we never were talking money like this before. We're talking a few hundred grand for a few minutes work. Do you know what that means? We could pay off the house, the cars, and invest in some stock, maybe open a business and then just sit back and watch our money work for us while we're down in the islands somewhere sippin' Mai Tais on my time and enjoying the good life."

"Sounds like a plan but is it really worth it Chaz.? I mean we have each other and really what more is there? I remember when we had that little one bedroom flat over on East Hudson and you couldn't find a happier couple. Do you remember how we used to wrap the aluminum foil around the end of the antenna so we could get one or two channels on TV? Remember that old radio that you used to have to walk around the room and hold over your head to get WBLS to come in. You used to hold that radio in one hand and wrap your other arm around me and we'd slow dance until it lost its signal?"

Chaz smiled.

"Life was so much simpler then," he said shrugging.

"And ain't no reason it has to be complicated now."

"So, what you're saying is that you don't want me to take the fight?"

"You know I don't. All the money in the world ain't worth me jeopardizing my baby's life or health. You and I are different Chaz. I believe that when you play with fire on a consistent basis your numbers eventually gonna come up and if you ain't no firemen chances are your ass is gonna get burned. And so far you've been both lucky and blessed but you can't continually play with fire without getting burned. And I think that's what you're doing."

"Ramia, trust me. You know I know what I'm doing. You don't get to be world champ if you're not good. And I'm not just good. I'm the best."

"Don't let that little leather belt go to your head champ. As easily as God blessed you he can take it away."

"I know. You're right. All I'm saying is that I'm known for being a defensive fighter. Most boxers have a hard time finding me let alone hitting me."

"You can't live in the past Chaz."

"And what's that supposed to mean?"

"I was there tonight remember and I had to leave after watching the so-called defensive fighter get his teeth rattled by that kid on several occasions and he wasn't close to Hector Pepito or any of those guys you went to war with back in the day. He was average but you made him look good because you aren't the same boxer that won the title five years ago."

"So you say."

"Yeah, so I say but I'm your wife and I'll tell you the truth and you know that Chaz. I'm not Mike who's trying to live his dreams through you. And I'm sure not one of those others that only looks at you as a meal ticket. They don't give a fuck about you as long as you line their pockets. Come on Chaz! Wake up! Most of those that tag along with you are only interested in what you can do for them and you know it. You can't be that naive that you don't recognize that."

"Are you finished?" Chaz asked knowing that Ramia was telling the truth.

"Yeah, I'm finished but you go ahead and take the fight. It's always been your dream to see your name up in lights and share center stage so you go ahead but I'll tell you this. If you even mention another fight after this and I don't care if they offer you ten million I'm leaving you. Do you understand?"

"I think I do." Chaz said taking the tiny woman in his arms and embracing her tightly.

"You'd better do more than think you do 'cause I'm serious. I'm leaving and taking the baby with me."

"Chaz stepped back and looked at Ramia with surprise.

"What baby?"

"Your son Chaz."

"Hold up. What are you talking about woman?"

"I was keeping it as a surprise 'til after the fight. What do you think the champagne was for? I thought we'd celebrate the closing of one chapter and the beginning of another."

"So, what are you saying Ramia? Are you saying that I'm going to be a father?"

Ramia smiled.

"I hope so if someone doesn't kill you first."

"Stop playing?"

And with one quick scoop Chaz had her in his arms swinging her around in circles like a seven year old schoolgirl.

"Oh my God. I'm going to be a father."

The two made love so many times that night that they lost count. And when it was over Chaz was ready to give up his title and declare all one hundred and eight pounds of Ramia the new undisputed champ. In the morning the two lay in each other's' arm until long after daybreak when Ramia heard a knock at the door.

"Mike said he's here to take you to the hospital." Ramia said shaking Chaz and staring at him angrily. "I thought you told me nothing was wrong with you."

"Nothing is," Chaz lied. "It's just a precautionary measure to make sure nothing's broken. We stopped by docs on the way home last night and he said I looked fine but wanted to take some x-rays just to be sure. You know how doc is. He'd rather be safe than sorry."

"Save the b.s. Chaz. What is supposed to be broken?"

"They're looking at my jaw but I'm telling you it's fine."

"So why are they looking at your jaw? Why did they just pick your jaw over the other parts of your body?"

"Well, the kid hit me a pretty good shot."

"I remember. Your legs buckled. That's why I left."

"Yeah, I give him credit. It was a good shot and it stung a little more than usual so I mentioned it to Mike after the fight and he took me to see doc who couldn't find anything but told me he wanted to make certain so he wants to take x-rays."

"Are you sure that's all."

"Positive baby." Chaz said getting up and grabbing an old pair of sweats lying across a chair and slipping them on before kissing the tiny woman on the cheek and making his way towards the front door.

"Morning pops," Chaz said greeting the old man.

"You seem to be quite chipper this morning. Guess that means Ramia took the news pretty well?" he inquired.

"Better than even I expected but after this fight I'm done."

The old man smiled.

"Did you make that decision or did she?"

"To tell you the truth pops I'd made the decision before the last fight. I was going to tell you last night but you seemed so excited over the whole HBO thing and I started thinking about the money so…"

"Well, I can't blame you. I'm just glad to know that you're smart enough to get out while you're still on top. Most fighters don't have the sense enough to get out while they're on top."

Chaz couldn't remember how many times he'd been in St. Mary's but it was certainly more than he cared to recall. His wife's words reverberated in his ears and as he waited to be x-rayed he knew that she was right.

"There's something else pops."

"I'm all ears Chaz."

"Ramia told me that I'm going to be a father," Chaz said smiling broadly.

"Well, congratulations son," the old man said grabbing Chaz and hugging him tightly. "I was wondering when you two were gonna make me a grandfather."

"Says she wants a father for the baby not a vegetable."

"Makes sense but you gotta understand that women are overly cautious. If you're in the best shape of your life the chances of you getting hurt are between slim and none. You just follow my directions and you'll be fine Chaz."

"I hear ya but this is my last fight pops no matter what happens."

"Anything you say Chaz. What can I say? You've provided me with the best twenty years any man could have asked for. Truth is a man couldn't have asked for a better son than you've been. The good Lord blessed me when he placed you in my life. And I'm not just saying that. I mean that from the bottom of my heart son."

"Thanks pops."

"No, thank you son."

The pretty little red-haired nurse appeared in front of Chaz at that very moment and Chaz never comfortable with his emotions was glad she'd appeared when she did.

"The doctor will see you now now Mr. Martinez," she said in an attempt to flirt with the young man. It wasn't the first time and Chaz now accustomed to it ignored her as usual and followed her into the room.

"I'm gonna run down to the cafeteria and grab some coffee. If you get out before I get back wait for me here."

Chaz nodded and continued to follow the nurse down the long hallway.

"Morning doc."

"Chaz. How are we feeling this morning?"

"Pretty good all things considered."

"How's the jaw?

"A little sore but I've felt worse."

"Well, that's good," the doctor replied taking Chaz's lower jaw in his hand and touching it gingerly and finding nothing out of place. "Like I said last night I can't find anything out of place but I want you to go down to Room 204 and let them take a couple of x-rays and as soon as I get the results I'll give you a call."

"Thanks doc."

An hour or so Chaz sat in the bathtub of the Jacuzzi and let the hot water bubble over his sore body. The phone rang and Chaz reached over to the commode, grabbed the phone and heard doc's voice on the other end.

"Well, son I was wrong. It happens you know," he laughed. "The x-rays show a hairline fracture. It's almost two small to see but it's there nonetheless."

Chaz heard the doctor's words but his thoughts were elsewhere. He was in line to defend his title in less than three months and a fracture of any kind could postpone the bout or cancel it and this was his chance of a lifetime. The payday alone would set him straight and if he handled his money well he'd never ever have to worry again about money.

"So what are you saying doc? You know I have a bout in three months. Probably the biggest bout of my career."

"And payday too."

"Yeah, that too. So, give me your professional opinion. Will I be able to go or not?

"Well in my professional opinion and if I were your trainer and manager I'd postpone the fight and allow you to heal properly."

"So you're saying that I need to call the fight off?"

""That's a no-brainer Chaz. You're risking permanent damage and possible disfigurement if you were to take the fight."

"I hear you doc."

"That's not all though Chaz. I think a lot of the pain you're experiencing is not from your jaw but from your nose. I don't know why you didn't know but your nose is broken as well. So, in response to your question you have a dual issue and there's no way you should take the fight as scheduled. If you can put it off for say six months I think you'll be good to go."

"Six months?" Chaz said incredulously. "C'mon doc you know how the game works as well as anyone. And you know if I pulled out or tried to get a postponement they'd just replace me and this is the chance of a lifetime. I could retire after this payday."

"I understand Chaz but as your doctor I'm not concerned with anything other than your health and although you may go in there and score a first round knockout without ever being touched it's my job to warn you that it's not in your best interest to take the fight. Your health comes first in my eyes and I know it's the payday of a lifetime but what good is the money if you can't spend it."

"I hear ya doc. You sound like Ramia."

"And I think anybody that loves you will agree."

"I gotcha doc. And thanks for calling. I'll be in touch. Oh, and one more thing doc..."

"Yeah, sure anything for you Chaz."

"Could you keep this on the down low?"

"Do I have a choice? It's called doctor patient confidentiality. As a doctor I'm not permitted to divulge any information on a patient without his consent."

"I know doc but I know how close you and pops are and like I said this is the chance of a lifetime and I don't want to blow it."

"So, you're going ahead with the fight?"

"Got to."

"Well, just for the record you know you'll be taking the fight a.ma.

"What's a.m.a doc?"

"A.m.a. is against medical advice."

"I know doc. I know."

"Okay, Chaz it's your decision and congratulations again on last night."

"Thanks again doc," Chaz said hanging up the phone and leaning back in the lukewarm water. The decision was a no-brainer. He had to take the fight. But one last fight would neither make him nor break him. He wasn't one of those boxers who loved the fight game. He owed everything to the game but he wasn't one of those that sought the spotlight. No, it was pops that had to push him out there to accept the endorsements, the interviews, the limelight. If he had his choice he was just as happy to just hang out with Ramia at the local drive-in.

During the following weeks Chaz did little more than lie around the house glued to the television relaxing. He'd driven down to Atlantic City where he and Ramia got a suite at the Regents Casino. In all his time living in New York he'd never been to Atlantic City and as Ramia had a penchant for the slots Chaz thought he'd indulge her. Giving her a few hundred dollars he left her to the slots and headed to the beach where he logged his four miles and after returning to the room to shower he'd meet Ramia down in the casino and listen to her tell stories of how'd she'd almost hit or been up before losing everything. It tickled him to listen to the same story he'd heard for eleven years and wondered why his wife so logical in most things could never understand that casinos weren't set up to do anything but take her money. Still, she seemed happier than at any other time pressing buttons and losing his hard earned money so he said little. At least she wasn't one of those degenerate gamblers that would sit there and spend their last knowing good and well that they had bills to pay and the baby needed shoes.

They would then go to lunch together before Ramia would return to gamble some more and Chaz would grab a cold one and be content to sit on the boardwalk and observe the tourists.

Returning home Sunday evening both seemed exhausted. Monday Chaz would begin training in earnest and so Ramia made it a point that she received all the loving she could knowing that it would be three months before she'd have the opportunity again.

As always the lovemaking was nothing short of sensational and wrapped in Chaz's arms Ramia slept soundly never even hearing Chaz's groans when he woke at four thirty in the morning. He was sore beyond belief. He'd felt this way more often than he cared to remember but this time it was different. He couldn't remember for the life of him who he'd fought or why he was so sore. His body ached as he stood trying to clear the sleep and cobwebs from his head. Glancing around the room for his sweatshirt his eyes fell on his wife, all one hundred and eight pounds of her and smiled as he bowed to the new and undisputed featherweight champ. She had won again and he had to smile. He'd grown accustomed to her winning every round and it always ending in a TKO.

The mornings after were always the same and he had to smile as he realized he'd never ever really been a match for her in the bedroom.

Chaz hit the long winding driveway running. If there were one thing about training that he didn't mind it was the roadwork. In fact, it was perhaps the only part of training that he really enjoyed. It hadn't been that way in the beginning. But after sometime he relished the fact that this was the only time he could be alone with his thoughts.

When his mother had passed after a long bout with breast cancer this was where he'd come to terms with her death. And when he found out his baby sister, who held a special place in his heart had contracted AIDS after a long bout with heroin it had been here that he had sought solace. And even today with doc's warning and a new baby on the way he welcomed the roadwork. He needed this time to clear his head and sort things out.

Chaz thought long and hard about doc's warning and even though he knew doc was right he knew he had to take the fight. His jaw still ached and he'd refused doc's advice on having his jaw wired shut to hasten the healing process so as not to alarm Ramia but Lord knows it certainly didn't seem like it was getting any better and he'd been forced to listen and merely groan an uh huh to what most of what his wife chattered on about over the past few weeks. And he could only imagine what would happen once he started sparring again and got caught with a good punch or a head butt in the clinch.

His nose wasn't as much of a factor and he couldn't count the times it had been broken before and he had simply put a face brace on and continued training. He could always tell Mike about the broken nose and the ol' man would limit his sparring partners from head hunting but even so an accidental head butt or someone just cinching and leaning on his jaw would have him wincing in pain. Still, if he told the ol' man about both his nose and jaw being broken the ol' man would most surely call the fight off no matter how much he wanted to see Chaz finally grab the spotlight he so richly deserved. He knew the ol' man loved him and would never let him jeopardize his health. No, this was one time he had to walk alone. Now he had the added responsibility of taking care of not only the ol'man, the gym and Ramia but a child as well.

Only a few years ago his mother had asked him to look after his younger sister and no matter how hard he tried he just didn't have the money to get her the help she truly needed. But that was then and this was now and he vowed that money would never again be an obstacle.

Climbing the steep hill that was his driveway he began to really push and was all but spent when he reached the palatial home. As much as he loved running it just wasn't quite as easy as it used to be. Still, Chaz knew that anything worth having one had to work for and so he pushed on. Flying through the backdoor he grabbed the tiny woman and squeezed her tightly pressing her to his sweaty body.

"Ooooh, Chaz!! Get off me with your sweaty stinky self," Ramia said feigning disgust.

"You didn't say that last night," Chaz laughed.

"Didn't want to hurt the champs' ego knowing how much you were trying to please me and all."

"So what are you saying? Are you trying to tell me it wasn't good?"

"I didn't say that but the whole time you were sweating and trying to please me I was thinking that you could probably bottle and market your lovemakin' as a new and improved sleep aid."

"Oh, no you didn't," Chaz laughed.

"Oh but I did," Ramia remarked as she took out a cup and cut out the biscuits before putting them on a greased cookie sheet and placed them in the oven.

"Now run upstairs and take a shower. The biscuits will be ready in a minute."

"I know you don't think you're gonna get off that easy."

"Oh, Chaz you know you know you're my everything. Now go on. Breakfast is almost ready and you know Mike will be here in twenty minutes. In twenty years he ain't never been late to pick you up."

Chaz grinned before grabbing the love of his life and hugging her once more before making his leave.

Bounding up the stairs he leaned over the bannister and shouted to Ramia.

"You know when I got up this morning I was trying to recall who I fought last night. My whole body was sore. And I said to myself whoever it was and I swear I couldn't remember but all I know is that the way I was feeling I must have lost my belt and there had to be a new middleweight champion."

"And what's that supposed to mean."

"I'm just saying that you kicked my butt."

"You're so full of it, Chaz."

"I'm dead serious. I woke up and was sore all over."

Ramia laughed.

"What you need is a new trainer. You're just out of shape is all."

"Is that right?"

"Absolutely and soon as you get this last fight behind you I have just the person in mind."

"And who would that be?"

"Well you may be the champ in the ring but I have some different rules in my arena. First and foremost there will be no more falling asleep before I'm finished with you. But let's take one thing at a time. Now would you please take your shower before Mike gets here?"

Chaz smiled. Mike called Ramia a whippersnapper and she was certainly all of that and more.

The warm water cascaded down on Chaz's chiseled frame and if it weren't for the smell of the homemade biscuits invading the bathroom Chaz may have remained right there until he heard Mike's truck pull up but if it was one thing he had a weakness for it was Ramia's homemade biscuits. Mama had never been one to share her recipes but the old woman loved Ramia almost as much if not more than Chaz did and had willingly shared the recipe and although Chaz thought it tantamount to sacrilege he had to admit that mama had nothing on Ramia in the kitchen.

Getting out of the shower he was not surprised to find his clothes laid out and his gym bag packed. Ramia had been doing this for years and today was no exception.

Chaz dressed quickly and headed downstairs where Mike sat waiting.

"Good thing you got down here when you did," Mike said.

"And why's that?" Chaz asked incredulously.

"Well, Ramia insisted on me having breakfast and after having a couple of biscuits I made her an offer to leave you and elope with me."

Chaz laughed.

"They are good aren't they?"

"Boy, I haven't had anything like them since my mother, rest her soul, made 'em for me when I was a boy no higher than this," Mike said holding his arm out.

Ramia smiled with pride.

"I asked Mike if he would be the baby's godfather. I hope you don't mind Chaz."

"Mind? Why would I mind? And?" Chaz said looking first at Ramia then at the old man.

"What could I say? Although looking at you I had to wonder if maybe there was someone else that could probably do a better job raising a child should something happen to either one of you."

"Ahhh pops looking at the job you did on Chaz it's hard to think that anybody could do a better job raising a child than you and that's why you were my first and only choice," Ramia said proudly. "You did a hell of a job on Chaz. I can remember when he was twelve or thirteen and I hated him. He was the baddest little kid in the whole school. Stayed in the principal's office and was just as bad in the streets when he got out of school…that is if he went to school and you changed all of that in a couple of months. Now he's a loving, humble, soft spoken middleweight champion of the world. What more could someone ask?"

"Well, I could ask that for once he'd be on time," the old man smiled as he sopped p the last of the gravy with his biscuit. "Damn these are good!!"

Back in the dilapidated gym a visitor would never have been able to tell the difference between Chaz, the middleweight champion of the world and the fourteen year old trying to learn how to duck and weave at doc's instruction. Doc was hard on them all and Chaz knowing this not only accepted it but thrived in the atmosphere. He'd long ago come to the understanding that the old man favored no one but wanted each to reach his full potential and simply be the best he could be.

Chaz had told him about his nose being broken on the ride over and was glad to hear him shout out to Billy Devlin that there were to be no head shots and only go to the body in the sparring session. Still, somewhat precarious Chaz stepped into the ring.

"What's up Billy?"

"Ain't nothin' Chaz. How you been man?"

"Chillin' you know. Just sitting back….Relaxing at the lounge with the old lady. Same ol' Same ol'."

"Livin' that good life."

"I'm making it. Trying to keep the lights on."

"Heard you had a little one on the way."

A smile a mile wide appeared on Chaz's face and he suddenly remembered the pain in his jaw.

"Yeah, man that's one of the reasons I'm taking this last fight. Ramia doesn't want me to take it and don't tell pops but I don't want to take it either. Went to see doc after the last fight with the kid and found out that he broke my jaw and my nose."

"And pops is still letting you fight?"

"I didn't tell him about my jaw just my nose so don't go too hard on me."

"What did doc say?"

"Told me to postpone the fight but I'm broke and with the baby coming I don't have a choice."

"Did you tell Ramia?"

"Hell no. She doesn't want me to take the fight as it is. Keeps talking about me getting a job, going to work and me getting out of the game."

"She may be right Chaz."

"I know she is. That's why win or lose this is my last fight."

"I know that's right. Here comes pops. You ready?"

"Yeah. Just go easy Billy."

"No problem. I'll keep it downstairs."

"I appreciate that man."

The days and weeks that followed went much the same way with Chaz stopping in to see doc every couple of weeks.

"Your nose is healing nicely Chaz but one good shot and you could be right back at square one. Have you been wearing the nose guard?"

"Yeah doc." Chaz lied.

"That's your best protection and will keep it in place until it completely heals. You still considering taking on this fight?"

"Got to doc."

"How long have I known you Chaz?"

"I don't know. Maybe fifteen or twenty year's doc… I think the first time I met you was when I broke my hand and pops brought me in to see you. I think I was thirteen at the time."

"And you're thirty now. And out of the boxers pops has brought to me my relationship with you is and always has been different. You have always been more than just a patient to me. You're like the son pops and I never had. If anything ever happened to you it would crush me and the old man."

"I'll be alright doc."

"Pops tells me your wife asked him to be godfather."

Chaz grinned.

"So you're going to be a father?"

"Yes sir. She's due in April."

"And how are you set financially?"

"I'm not doc. That's why it's so important that I take this fight and secure a future for my family."

"I kinda figured that boy but I think that your family would much rather have a husband and father around than financial security."

"I hear you doc."

"Well, Chaz if it'll make it any easier on you, me and the missus have a little saved up and it's yours if you need a loan to help you to transition from boxing to the real world. It would probably support you for a year or so or until you get on your feet."

Chaz felt the tears welling up in his eyes and had to fight them back before he could speak again.

"Doc, you don't know how much that means to me and you don't know much I appreciate that but I've made it through a hundred and something amateur and thirty three pro fights and I'll be okay for one last fight. And win or lose this fight should secure my family's future for a long time so thank you but no thank you doc. Trust me I've got this," Chaz said crouching and throwing out a left and a right that fell inches from doc's midsection.

Doc smiled and moved away.

"Have you told Ramia?"

"No."

"And don't you think you should?"

"No, it would just cause her to worry even more. And you know she worries when I'm perfectly healthy."

"Okay, Chaz. I guess there's nothing else for me to say. What I will need is for you to sign these papers saying that you're taking the fight AMA."

"AMA doc?"

"Yes, I told you before. This states that you're proceeding with the fight against medical advice from your doctor. That's just in case something, God forbid, does happen to you. They'll want an investigation and this is to protect me and says that I advised you not to take on the fight because of some medical concerns."

"Oh, c'mon doc. Don't you think you're being a little over dramatic?"

"Maybe and I sincerely hope so but it's merely a precautionary measure to protect me at this point."

"Okay, doc where do you want me to sign?"

Doc pointed and after signing and hugging doc tightly Chaz left the office and headed home. The smell of pinto beans and ham hocks greeted Chaz and he was only too happy to have chosen Ramia to be his wife. He could hardly imagine having married a woman who didn't know her way around the kitchen.

"Hey, baby."

"Hey sweetie. You're home early. What's up?"

"Can't a man take a little timeoff to spend with his wife?"

"I guess," Ramia replied looking puzzled. Chaz was as disciplined and dedicated as anyone she'd ever met and had never in all the time she'd known him given anything but a hundred percent when it came to preparing for a fight. Maybe because it was his last go round she mused. Maybe he was truly tired of the game.

"Okay, but that's not the Chaz Martinez that I know. And pops said it was okay for you to miss the day only a month before the fight."

"Well, actually I'm still training. I'm just not sparring until a week or two before the fight."

"Jaw must really be hurting my baby," Ramia said knowing full well that her husband always sparred in the last month of training if for nothing else than to sharpen his defensive skills and reflexes. "That doesn't even sound like pops," she said nonchalantly.

"If you must know pops and I sat down and decided that being that I'm an older fighter and have been in so many wars there's no need to take any unnecessary punishment at this stage of my career."

"Sounds good if you're talking to the media or someone who doesn't know you or pops but you're talking to me sweetheart. Now are you going to tell me the truth or not."

"That is the truth Ramia," Chaz said angry now that he couldn't get anything by her. Standing up from the table he grabbed the remote and headed for the living room.

"Don't you walk away from me Chaz Martinez."

Ramia never called Chaz by his full name unless she was angry and it gave Chaz moment for pause. Still, no matter how angry she got he wasn't telling her any more than he already had. There was no need for her to worry herself especially in her present condition.

"I just know you didn't just get up and walk in the other room with an attitude."

Chaz smiled and looked at the woman in front of him. For someone no more than five feet, if she was that, the little fireball of a woman had quite an imposing presence about her. When she and Chaz had first met she couldn't have been more than a hundred pounds dripping wet and over the next fifteen years she hadn't gained but a couple of pounds. And if Chaz had one gripe about his wife it was that she was too thin but no longer did he have to worry about that. In the first couple of months of her pregnancy she had picked up close to ten pounds and was by his standards as fine and voluptuous as they come.

"Come here baby," Chaz said reaching his arms out her.

"Don't come over here with that baby me crap. You tell me what's going on right now."

Chaz laughed.

"Baby, I don't know what you want me to tell you other than what I've already told you. What do you want me to do? You want me to make up something just to comfort you?"

"And that's what I've been doing. Have I ever lied to you Ramia?" Chaz said grabbing holding his wife's hands in his own and looking her straight in the eye.

"No."

"Listen Ramia. You know I've trained hard for every fight I've ever had and after more than twenty years in the game I think I have it pretty much down. Trust me baby. I'm okay. The only difference between then and now is I don't have much of a game plan this time around. I'm fighting that kid out of Philly I fought a couple of years ago. Oh what's his name? He was a real good prospect and on the come up when I fought him. Nice kid with his head on right. Oh, what's his name?"

"Miguel Garcia."

"Yeah that's him. Like I said he's a real good kid. I roomed with him in when we were in the Pan Am games about ten years ago."

"Didn't you beat him by KO a couple of years ago?"

"Yeah, knocked him out with a right hook. You got a good memory sweetie."

"Yeah I remember him 'cause he shook you a few times."

Chaz laughed.

"Well, that was then. I've come a long way since then."

"And I'm sure he has too."

"Whatever."

"Don't underestimate him Chaz."

"I'm not. Just trying to get in there, do some work and get on back home."

"I hear you talking but I want you to train like it's a title bout and you're hungry. And I want you to win Chaz."

"I'm surprised to hear you talking like that."

"Well, you know your future after boxing will pretty much depend on how you do in this fight. And it's sad to say that most people have short memories and won't remember much beyond what you did in your last fight. So, if any fight needs to stand out it should be this last one."

"Makes sense to me."

"So, get on back to the gym and I want you to train like you never have before. You've got less than three weeks left Chaz. I want you to make this fight the most memorable one of you career. And I'll take care of you after boxing is over. Will you do that for mommy papi?" she said moving into his arms.

"Anything for my sweetie pie," Chaz said bending over and kissing her on her forehead before picking up his duffel bag and heading for the silver grey Mercedes in the driveway.

On the way Chaz pondered the little woman's words. He had been taking the fight lightly and was purposely avoiding any contact after sparring with the new kid pops had brought in to spar with him last Friday. Unable to warn him about his jaw the kid caught him flush with a left hook to his broken jaw that left him sprawled on the canvas writhing in obvious pain. It wasn't the first time he'd been caught in a sparring session. There was always some young punk willing to risk it all to say he'd gone toe-to-toe with the champ and if word got out that he'd floored the champ and he had any boxing skills at all he'd certainly be a force to be reckoned with. But it was this punch, this chance encounter that convinced Chaz that the next time he took a punch like this it would be a payday. And so much to the chagrin of the old man he'd stopped sparring.

The old man was puzzled but said nothing. As long as he'd known Chaz he'd always followed his instruction up until this point but boxers were funny, superstitious to a fault and hardly predictable. And when faced with the idea of being forced into retirement with no alternatives, behavior such as Chaz's

wasn't at all that hard to predict. And with so many other promising young fighters in the ranks the old man had neither the time nor the energy to devote to an aging fighter with one fight left.

But as quickly as Chaz had departed the old dilapidated gym he reappeared, dressed quickly and stepped into the ring. Pops smiled seeing him back then continued on with the other boxers.

"Billy get in there with Chaz. Go three rounds as a southpaw. Charles when he finishes I want you in there next. And then Billy I want you for the last three rounds going only to the body."

Both boxers cognizant of Chaz's jaw refrained from going all out and kept much of their attack to the body much to the aging fighter's relief. When he finished sparring Chaz changed into his running shoes and headed for the streets.

"Whoa whoa whoa!! Pops shouted at the young man heading out the door. "Slow your roll."

"Yeah pops," Chaz said jogging in place.

"What's going on with you man?"

"Nothing pops. Why you ask?"

"Cause in all the time we've been together I can't ever remember you being openly defiant and disrespecting me in public the way you did today. And I ain't never seen you blow off training and walk out."

"Sorry pops. I apologize for that. I just got a lot on my mind is all."

"I'm just wondering if what's bothering you is on your mind or if it's something else."

"What do you mean?"

"I saw when that kid hit you the other day and you went down. It was a good shot but I've seen you take a lot better shots but I ain't never seen you go down like that in all the time we been together. I'm thinking that your jaw is in a lot worse shape than you've been letting onto."

"It's broke pops."

"What are you saying boy?"

"Got both my nose and jaw broken in the last fight."

"Did doc say that?"

"And he ain't never sayed nothing to me."

"He couldn't. Doctor patient confidentiality. Plus I made him promise not to say nothing."

"And he's still saying you can fight?"

"Well, he advised against me taking the fight and I told him I didn't have any choice. I had to take the fight so he made sign papers saying I'm fighting against his medical advice to make sure he wasn't responsible if anything were to happen to me."

"Wow! And all this time I thought you were smarter than that. Chaz, you don't know how long I've waited for this moment. I'm seventy four years old and I can honestly say I've waited a lifetime for this very day. But I ain't sending my first born off to war and I ain't sending you in the ring against a doctor's medical advice to see you hurt, maimed or permanently disfigured for either money or fame. You mean more than that to me," the old man stood up put an arm around Chaz's shoulder, before patting him on the back and making his way back into the sea of boxers.

Chaz left the gym and was almost sorry he'd said anything. And then following Ramia's instructions he hit the streets running. The weeks leading up to the fight followed in much the same way with Chaz not simply training but overtraining pushing himself to limits he'd never before pushed himself to in order to put himself in a position where people would wonder after the fight was over why he'd even considered retiring. He would put on the best show of his twenty year career and walk out of the ring the winner and still undefeated, and undisputed champion of the world.

"Goodness, me and my bigmouth. What is it my daddy used to say? Be careful what you wish for," Ramia remarked to no one in general.

"What are you talking about little lady?" Chaz grinned downing the pint of bottled water from the fridge before grabbing another and doing the same with it. Finishing the second he grabbed his wife and held her. Just think in two more days and it'll all be just a memory. We'll look back on these days when we sit holding our grandkids calling these the good old days."

"Picture that," Ramia laughed. "Our first one hasn't even been born yet and already you have us holding the grandkids."

"But what's this about being careful what you wish for?"

"A couple of weeks ago I mentioned that you should train like this was a title bout 'cause this is your last fight and the fight that you and everyone else would probably remember most and ever since I made that comment you seemed possessed. I mean you really took it to heart. I have never seen you train this hard."

Chaz smiled and dropped his head where his chin rested on top of hers. It was several moments before he spoke and she didn't have to look up for her to know he was thinking and going over his words deliberately before responding.

"You know so often when a man retires from something he loves it's because he's forced to retire either because of age, amidst scandal or controversy or waning skills. If anyone of those applies to me it most definitely is my skill waning but I want to defy the odds and look good and go out on top. I want to go out undefeated. I don't want people to think that I lost and was forced into retirement. I just want to go out strong on and on top."

Junior Johnson and Me

I ain't never liked Tracy. I don't care what the other fellows thought of him. Sure he had the latest Jordans and only wore the latest gear. Talkin' bout he couldn't wear nuthin' but Aeropostale or he'd break out in hives. He was so stuck on himself that it made my stomach turn. And the girls used to eat it up. All his talk about what he could do and nobody seemed to care or look at Tracy for what he really was and that was a big blow hard. Whenever he arrived on the set I always found a way to make my leave and find my way home. It was funny though no one could understand how Tracy could afford the clothes and gear he wore. Both his mom and dad worked at the turkey plant just like most of our folks.

In fact, the turkey plant was the only job in town and everyone's parents worked there but Tracy was the only one of us that could afford to wear that kind of gear. He had three brothers and none of them dressed like Tracy did. But it made him special to everyone but me. I didn't care and although I wanted new clothes I knew better than to mention it. My father and mother worked very hard to provide for my two brothers and me and they both made sure there was always a good meal on the table. And when the other boys in Raeford cut school to go and crop tobacco to get some new gear and games for their systems I knew that my place was right there in school or I'd have to answer to pa and after that one occasion where I snapped back at pa when I was about twelve I knew I didn't want to relive that ordeal ever again. 'Sides after seeing ma and pa come in after work smelling that awful smell of dead turkeys and just seeing how plumb wore out they'd be I believed pa when he told me the only way out was to get a good education. Sure most of my friends dressed a whole lot cooler than me but I believed pa when he told me that one day it would all pay off. And so I applied myself as best I could and hung in there no matter how rough things got with my classes. On the weekend I'd go and help pa pour concrete and lay brick and he would say how there's nothing better than a man with a trade. He said a man with a trade never had to depend on nobody when it came to making a living and supporting his own but himself. So, pa would work six or seven days a week and on Fridays when the turkey plant closed and all the other plant workers would be going to Big P's to cash their checks and getting a pint of this or a fifth of that. Pa would come home and hand his check to ma and go down in the cellar and grab a saw and a couple of two by fours and head outside and work on the fence posts that was starting to wear down or start making some repairs on the barn. He'd only recently purchased the farm we lived on and we had about thirteen acres or so and were the only Black family around that had a mortgage. Everybody was renting from the folks that owned the turkey plant but pa said as long as you was renting from them and shopping at their store you were basically working for free and he wasn't going to have no parts of that. We grew our own vegetables and raised a couple of farm animals so we always had food but pa still struggled to pay the bills and make ends meet so I never could dress the way Tracy did and I wasn't going to bother pa as hard as he worked about some clothes when he had five mouths to feed.

Now Junior Johnson and me were best friends and had been ever since kindergarten when he used to be my next-door neighbor. He'd moved away since then but we still remained best friends. Junior and I were in the same grade and in the same classes along with Tracy but unlike me Junior liked Tracy or at least appeared to like him. He used to tell me that I was jealous of him but what was there to be jealous of. Yeah, his clothes were nicer than mine and yeah, all the girls liked him but besides that there was no reason for me to be jealous. At least there wasn't in my eyes.

Junior and I were pretty much inseparable in grade school being that we were next door neighbors and used to walk to school and all but now since we were in high school and all these new kids were bussed in from the other schools it seemed like Junior just wanted to be apart of the crowd. A lot of dudes were like that so I really couldn't blame Junior. To me though it didn't make all that much difference. The friends I'd grown up with and gone to grade school was all-pretty cool with me and I had a few close friends, close like Junior and me was. Now that's not to say that I didn't meet a few new kids that were real cool and I even met a few breezy's that I though were cute but for most part I stayed with my old friends. But not Junior. Junior wanted to be just like Tracy. Junior really wanted to be cool. And so more and more he started to hang around with Tracy and his crew and less with me and all the fellas he'd grown up with.

Anyways, I was working out in back of the farm one day repairing some fence posts with my pa and he made the remark that he hadn't seen Junior around much since school had started and so I told him how Junior had chosen to be cool and I guess me and my friends weren't cool enough anymore because we didn't dress in the latest fashions or have the latest sneakers.

"Does it bother you son that you don't have the latest fashions son like some of the other kids you go to school with?"

I had in no way meant for pa to think that I was suffering or unappreciative. After all, I knew he worked all the time trying his best to provide for our family and was a good father and a good man besides. And even though Junior's father and mother worked at the same turkey plant as my dad his parents spent every weekend at the bar, drinking and carousing with the other lowlifes who didn't want nothing much out of life. In fact that's why Junior had to move away in the first place because his parent's hadn't taken care of business and had fallen behind on the rent so bad ol' man Buzby put them out. And from what I heard from Junior they was getting' ready to be put out again. Said his momma and daddy was hittin' the bottle all the time now. And his mom had even lost her promotion for missin' work so much. Nah I didn't care much about clothes or all the other things those other kids had. I liked my life just the way it was. I liked the fact that my mom and dad worked hard and made damn sure that my brothers and sisters never went hungry and were always there for us. My dad would take us hunting and trapping with him when the first frost hit and take the whole family camping when the first flowers bloomed in the spring. I couldn't have asked for more. And every now and then he'd take the whole family to the beach for a day or two. So, it wasn't hard for me to answer him when he asked me if I thought he was doing enough or if I missed having all the new clothes and toys kids my age had.

"Nah pa. I'm good", and just to change the subject so pa wouldn't spend too much time worrying whether he was being a good father or not I changed the topic to one of his favorite subjects. Camping.

"Did you see the new catalog that came in the mail today?"

"No. Who's it from?"

"Cabela's"

"Oh yeah. Anything good in it?"

He continued to hammer away but I knew my father and soon as he'd finished mending the fence he'd head straight for the catalog. My father could barely read and write but loved to leaf through hunting and fishing catalogs or anything to do with the outdoors so I knew just how to get his mind off of me not having new clothes or him not being the best father he could be.

"Anything new in there?"

"Well, I was looking at this one tent that has three rooms and can hold up to ten people."

"Is that right? And what are they asking for that?"

"Well, the retail price is three seventy nine but they're only asking two and a half on sale."

"May just have to look into that," he mumbled through clenched teeth that held three or four nails.

When we'd finished he and I walked back up to the house where mom had prepared a dinner that included a pot roast, some mashed potatoes, and some fresh string beans from the garden. A large pitcher of fresh squeezed lemonade topped it off and we all ate heartily. When dinner was over and I finished my chores I asked pa if I could head up to the park and after inquiring about my homework I knocked on my friend Jamie's door and headed on up to the park.

It was crowded as usual but at this time of evening there were few kids here or mother's pushing strollers. At eight o'clock it was usually just us teenagers who were hanging out and trying to act all grown up. Some would hang in small groups and just be loud talkin' and cursing and trying to get attention. Sometimes they'd stand in a small circle and smoke a blunt or pass a cheap bottle of wine around until somebody got sick or too high and had to be escorted home. But me, I didn't have time for that mess and after pa had let me have a sip of his corn liquor which he only took out for special occasions like Christmas I ain't never had no yearnin' for no liquor. Truth is I can't ever remember being that sick in my entire life. I mean I threw up everywhere and two days later I still had the runs. Now the mere thought of alcohol makes me sick. With smoking it was the same way. A man my pa worked with had just had his first child and gave my dad a cigar as a sort of congratulatory thing and my dad had laid it down without smoking it and there it sat for a few days until me with my bright self picked it up one day when my parents weren't home. And me being somewhat curious and somewhat dumb, I have to admit, found some matches and tried to smoke it. Needless to say the same thing occurred except this time my pa whooped me good for doing something I had mo business doing even though I think the dizziness and throwing up was a good enough lesson in itself.

So, by this time I had come to the realization that if smoking and drinking meant being cool then I was just going to be one un-cool cat. And so me and Jamie mainly went up to the park to play ball and being that I was just a tad under six four and Jamie about six feet and we were both on the basketball team and everybody knew it and respected us for that nobody really messed with us for not being one of the cool guys. We didn't play ball all of the time though. Sometimes we just went to hang out and watch the girls and that's what we were doing on this particular night when I saw Junior and Tracy hanging out over where the old men used to hang out. Every now and then we'd see Junior's daddy hanging out with the rest of the winos from the plant and I had to wonder how Mr. Johnson had gotten so bad. But being that Junior wasn't worried about it it made no sense for me to worry about it. Still, the first couple of times I saw Mr. Johnson in this state it affected me so that I had to come home and ask my pa what happened to Mr. Johnson that had made him slip so low and pa couldn't say much more than 'life affects different men in different ways' which at the time made no sense to me but I let it go nonetheless. But to see Junior over there with Tracy where the older men did their bidding made no sense at all to me 'til Jamie pulled my coat about the whole drug thing.

"Remember when we was in seventh and eighth grade and they used to cut school to go crop tobacco and make a few extra dollars, Chris?"

I nodded.

"Now they don't work nearly as hard. All they do is get them a package and feed the dopefiends."

"What you saying?" I asked halfway between bewildered and stupid.

"All those ol' niggas over there are either on that crack or dope or trying to drink themselves into the grave. And your little friend Junior is one of the main suppliers."

"Are you trying to tell me that Junior is selling dope?"

"C'mon Chris, don't tell me that you're that much of a lame that you didn't know? How you think he started getting all fly and he ain't but sixteen. Nigga can't fill out an application let alone hold a job and that's if there were some jobs to hold here in Raeford. From what I hears the boys on the come up and rising fast. Say he was movin' so fast that he and Tracy almost got into it."

"So what's he selling?" I asked still somewhat shocked.

"Well, Tracy was selling dope cause the way he tells it dopefiends are bad but not as bad as crackheads and hooked Justin up with his supplier so Junior could corner the market on crack since he a lot bigger and when those crazy crackheads started getting out of line Junior could put them right back in line. He was supposed to take care of that aspect while Tracy concentrate on selling heroin but Junior got to a point a couple of months ago where he decided that he was going to horn in on Tracy's business and sell dope too. And that's just what he did until we went to Malik's party and Tracy found out the rumours were true and caught Junior selling to one of his customers. I wasn't there but from what I heard Tracy pulled a nine on Junior in front of everybody and told Junior that if he ever caught him selling to one of his customers again he'd shoot him like a bitch."

"And what did Junior do?"

"Well, it looks like he did what Tracy told him and went back to selling just crack but the boys got a little crew now and from what I understand he and all of his boys stay strapped now. And they seem to be getting along pretty good now but if you know Junior he don't never forget nothing and if I was Tracy I'd steady be looking over my shoulder."

"You really think Junior would do something?"

"The Junior you know would never do nothing like he planning and I guess that's why you looking all surprised but I don't think you know this Junior. The Junior I'm talking about would stab his own momma. He the one that got his own daddy strung out."

"Don't say no shit like that."

"I ain't lying. His father's so strung out on crack he hardly goes to work anymore. Junior put him out of the house and has taken over caring for his mother and brothers and sisters. He's the man now. So, everyone figures it's just a matter of time before he makes his move and takes over the whole shit. Tracy's days are numbered."

"Damn Jamie. I guess I'm a little bit out of the loop."

"And it's a good thing you are. But don't let the fly gear fool you. Them boys days are numbered. Trust."

I laughed.

"What's so funny?"

"It's just that my pa was asking me earlier what happened to Junior and I told him he was one of the cool kids now and didn't have time to hang out with an unfortunate, lame like me."

"And what did your pa say?"

"My pa wanted to know if not having any new clothes bothered me."

"And?"

"And sometimes it does but I don't want to put any more pressure on my pa than he already has. He works hard enough as it is just trying to provide for me and my brothers and sisters. But now that I know how Tracy and Junior get theirs I don't feel half bad. If I never have shit I'm not going that route to get some. You feel me" "I hear you my brother," Jamie said before pointing over to the basketball courts where Lea was dribbling around Nicole and trying to shoot a three pointer from half court. Both girls were giggling madly and having a ball.

"Stop fouling me. You see I'm trying to shoot."

"Ain't nobody fouling you heifer. If you could get them forty four D's out of the way you might be able to get a shot off," Nicole laughed.

"Go to hell you flat-chested bitch."

Chris and Jamie watched the two girls antics and could only shake their heir heads.

"Lea is one fine breezy," Chris said matter-of-factly, his mind still on Jamie's depiction of Junior.

"You ain't never lied."

Still affected by the recent revelation Chris focused his eyes on the two girls on the court before turning to Jamie and asking rather naively.

"Do you think me talking to Junior will make a difference?"

"Make a difference as far as what?" Jamie asked incredulously.

"I mean do you think if I talked to him about selling that poison he might reconsider. C'mon you know growing up Junior was always the one that had a conscious and didn't want to see anyone hurt or suffering." "That was a long time ago Chris. Junior's watched his father and mother battle alcohol and drugs and almost completely abandon him and his little brothers and sisters. I guess he just got tired. When your own parents turn their backs on you I guess it's pretty easy to give up hope on the rest of the world if you know what I mean. And that boy ain't the same boy we grew up with. Believe that son. It's like he changed overnight. He's cold now. Hard. You know the type. He just don't give a fuck about nothing or nobody. He'd just as soon rob and shoot you as the next man. It don't matter that he grew up with you or that you were next-door neighbors and best friends. The boy's shut down completely. You know anyone who can sell his own father crack don't give a damn about anybody or anything. I'm telling you this nigga ain't got no conscience no more. It's sad really."

"I gotta try though. I wouldn't be a friend if I didn't. Besides ain't no future in what he's doing."

"You right about that but you can't tell him about that. He 's doing more than his parents are and taking care of his little brothers and sisters and still getting paid so how you gonna argue with that?"

"I don't know Jamie but I gotta try. Junior's too good a guy to get caught up in some shit like that."

"Okay, man. You do what you think is best. All I'm gonna say is talk to your pa first and see what he says. And if you still decide to spit some knowledge to Junior come get me first. I don't trust him. He's a snake if ever I saw one."

"I think I'll do just that."

Just then Lea and Nicole strolled over looking no better for the wear. It was clear their attempts at hoops had worn both girls out. Lea took a seat on the bleachers next to Chris intertwining her arm in his and making sure to lean over just enough for her breasts to brush against him.

"So what's up guys? You're just sitting here chillin'. You ain' hoopin' today?"

"Nah, we just sittin' here kickin' it," Jamie responded as Nicole slid up next to him.

"So what's the topic for the day?"

"Ain't nothin' we was just kickin' it about Junior and Tracy. My boy Chris was sitting here saying that he didn't know that Junior was dealing."

"Where you been Chris? Everybody knows that. He's been dealing since eighth grade. He used to sell a little weed here and there but from what I hear he's selling everything now. That's why Tracy pulled a gun on him at Chavelle's party. Remember?"

"I wasn't there," Chris replied.

"Oh, that's right. You sure weren't. That's the night you told me you were coming and never showed aand I waited all night for you."

Chris smiled.

"Had a few things to take care of."

"You always have something to do when I ask you to do something with me. If I didn't know any better I'd get the feeling that you didn't like me or were scared of me."

Again Chris smiled. He really liked Lea. But he didn't have any money to take her out and romance her the way she should be and until he did he thought it best to just leave her alone. And the truth of the matter was that he was a little afraid of her. He'd never been with a girl in that way and had to admit that no matter how many issues of Playboy and Hustler he leafed through he had no earthly idea of what to do when it came to girls. And being that Lea was one of the more popular girls and was from the Bottoms he was sure she had experience and although he would break out in cold sweats just thinking about her fine ass he didn't dare expose the fact that he was still a virgin and had little or knowledge when it came to things like making love or having sex. He was sure she could she could teach him but she could always turn around and laugh at the fact that he didn't know and he'd be the laughing stock of the whole school. Not that he had any reputation for anything other than his skills on the basketball court but he sure didn't want that tarnished by being considered a lame.

"Hey Lea, I've got to get home. You know it's a school night and my mom likes me to be home by ten."

"I'm ready. Chris is playing hard to get as usual so there's no need to hang around here. You know Chris, my mom says those who play hard to get don't get got."

Jamie smiled.

"Why don't you go ahead and give her a taste Chris so she'll stop crying all the time?"

"Yeah Chris why don't you take my girl out," Nicole concurred. "I'm so tired of hearing her fussing about why you won't ask her out when every senior boy has already cracked and she's sitting here pining away waiting on you to pop the question."

"Shut up heifer. See that's why I hate telling you anything. 'Cause you can't keep your big mouth shut."

Chris blushed. He stood up.

"C'mon Jamie let's walk these two home before Mrs. Brown comes down here looking for her," he laughed.

The foursome paired up and Lea slowed the pace so she could have Chris all to herself.

"Seriously though Chris, I know you like me. I see the way you look at me in homeroom and in class. But you never speak to me outside of a 'what's up Lea'. What's up with that? Your eyes tell me you're feeling me but you never try to push up or nothing. And you know I'm feeling you. I think that's pretty obvious and if it wasn't big mouth Nicole let the whole thing out the bag a minute ago. So, what's up Chris"

She still had her arm intertwined with his like young lovers do and Chris could feel his palms sweating and his heart race under her barrage of questions.

"I hope it's not just because I'm from the Bottoms or anything like that. You know there are some nice girls that live there. They're not all fast and loose."

"I never said that."

"I'll have you know I'm still a virgin. Well, that is until the right guy comes along. But all the boys I know look at me and I don't even have to ask. I already know that all they want to do is hit and quit it so they can run around and say that they've had me. And that ain't happening."

"And how do you know I don't want the same thing."

"I wish. I can't get the time of day from you. Sometimes I feel like I'm invisible around you."

Chris laughed.

"Hurry up slowpokes. My mother's gonna kill me if I'm late again," Nicole shouted back.

"Believe me you're not invisible Lea. But between babysitting my little brothers and sisters, school and basketball practice I just don't have time for anything else. It's not you Lea. I wish I did have time for a steady girl."

"Well, make time silly. How about if I come over and help you with your brothers and sisters? We could do homework together. I really could use help in Ms. Glover's class. She's a bitch and she hates me. I mean absolutely hates me. But she loves some Chris. You can do no wrong in there. Are you sure you're not tappin' that. I see the way she looks at you."

"You're crazy," Chris laughed. "But on the real though with all the guys you have trying to push up on you why would you choose me?"

"That's just it. They're all the same. You, on the other hand, are different and I like that. I like you. Isn't that enough?"

"I suppose."

"You suppose? Goodness don't sound so enthusiastic but then I guess you're used to having girls ask you out everyday big time basketball star."

Chris laughed and squeezed Lea's tiny shoulders. They were arriving at Nicole's house now.

"So, I'll see you tomorrow after school?"

Chris nodded.

"It's a date then," Lea said grinning from ear-to-ear.

"It's a date," Chris replied as Lea reached up and kissed him gently on the cheek.

He had to admit that he couldn't remember ever feeling this good but not wanting to seem too anxious turned to Lea and said.

"Make it around five I have to see Junior first."

"You need to leave Junior alone Chris. I know you two used to be best friends but he's really turned out to be bad news. The best thing you can do to help him and yourself is to leave him alone. He really is bad news." "I tried to tell him that but Saint Christopher, patron saint of the mentally insane things he can help that fool out," Jamie interrupted.

"Five o'clock it is then," Lea said smiling before reaching up and pulling Chris' head down and kissing him smack dab on the mouth this time before turning quickly and walking away.

Chris couldn't remember ever having felt better and the rest of the night and the next day seemed all a blur. He'd bumped into Junior that morning and told him he needed to holler at him after school and Junior agreed to meet him out front as soon as school dismissed but said it had to be quick because he had a previous engagement.

Chris knew that Jamie was supposed to meet him but there was no need for that despite what Jamie and Lea had said. He and Junior went too far back.

The dismissal bell rang at three o'clock sharp and Chris immediately regretted his decision to meet Junior when he caught a glimpse of fine ass Lea stroll by with Nicole.

"Five o'clock baby? Didn't get cold feet and change your mind did you?"

"Not a chance," he replied.

Damn he thought glancing at her. She looked even better than she had the previous night. It was early September and the weather was unusually warm for this time of year. Lea wore a black halter-top with white shorts and some white gladiator sandals accentuating her tight, round booty and thick mocha legs. He should have been walking with her instead of meeting Junior's wanna be thug ass.

Just then Chris glanced toward the corner where he'd agreed to meet Junior and saw four or five of his crew standing there conducting business as usual. He walked up as he saw Junior approach and give them their daily instructions. Their eyes met and Junior smiled broadly. It was genuine and Junior wondered how the two had grown so apart. If there had been one person he could always count on even when mom and dad had traded him in for substances at the time unbeknownst to him Chris had always remained his constant. And now there was absolutely no one he could talk to, or trust. He blamed himself for letting his best friend slip away but was glad Chris had come looking for him today. Much as he hated to admit it he needed his best friend. These niggas on the corner would just as soon do him in for a little extra cheddar than one of the fiends he served. They couldn't be trusted. In fact, there was no one he could trust anymore except for Chris. Chris would never get in the game. He was too smart for that besides his pops would kill him if he even got wind of him being associated with drugs. Still, he could get his boy some new gear. He remembered when they were younger and used to spend their time dreaming and window shopping and pretending they'd one day grow up and dress like some of the older cats in the hood that seemed to have it going on. He was sure his boy would love to have some of the same gear he was now wearing. He was just too afraid to put in the work needed to get it. That was it. He'd grab a ride and get away from this little one horse town and take his boy shopping. Maybe they'd grab a bite to eat and relive old times.

The two boys were a few paces apart when Junior's cell phone went off. He stopped to take the call which always meant a sale when a late model black Dodge Charger came screaming around the corner. At the close of the school day this wasn't unusual as most of the little White kids whose parents had money drove to school and would always make a scene showing off for their little girlfriends but today was somehow different as a hail of bullets from an automatic weapon filled the air along with the squealing of tires. It was pure chaos as teens ducked and ran and hit the ground in sheer panic. When it was over a tear dripped from Junior's eyes as he stood over his best friend.

LEA

She'd gotten the tragic news. Who hadn't? The school had been in an uproar for months after the shooting death of star basketball forward Chris Brown. The papers ran articles condemning everything from the rampant drug use and selling near schools to the increase in violence as a direct result of the increased drug traffic.

The small town of Raeford was only now starting to settle down in the aftermath of the shooting. The killers had never been apprehended and after a while life went on as usual in the small town. Well, that was life went on as usual for everyone that was except for Lea. Lea McMurray had a hard time understanding why God had taken such a sweet, sensitive, boy who was so young and in the prime of his life. She had a hard time dealing with the whole affair. It was the first time in her life that she'd ever been in love. And she knew he loved her. He was the only good thing in her life. She and Chris had made a pact to meet that very day and now this.

Life had changed after his death. Her grades dropped and she lost interest in almost everything including school. Most of her girlfriends were interested in shopping now and dating frequently but not Lea. Well, that was until Jason bumped into her at the local 7/11. She'd seen Jason around. It was hard not to. Raeford was such a small town but she'd never really paid any attention to him. He with all his flash and bling and swag was just not her type. Besides he was older—too old for her. And if it was one thing she knew she didn't need it was a drug dealer. There was just no future in it. Her older brother Jeremy had tried it and was now doing a six year bid. Her parents had been heartbroken when they first found out and then he started to dabble and eventually gotten hooked and was soon robbing and stealing anything and everything he could get his hands on. When he'd been arrested and sentenced to a six year bid both mommy and daddy breathed a deep sigh of relief that would at least know where their son was now. And the monthly visits to the jail almost certainly beat a visit to the morgue. Lea saw and recognized the pain that drugs could bring a family and had even come to see the by-products when Chris was killed. No Lea wanted no parts of drugs or those in the game and that included Jason. Besides, like she said he was way to old for her. Jason had to be at least twenty or twenty one and the Lexus he sported certainly wasn't typical of anyone that worked in the turkey plant. Still, she never saw him at any of the popular drug spots or hanging out with the rest of the dope boys.

"What's up shorty?" he said passing her in the cookie aisle of the tiny market.

"Hey," she responded not trying to be rude.

"Sweet tooth got you too I see," he said never taking his eyes off of the cookies finally settling on a box of Lorna Doones.

"I love me some Lorna Doones," he mused. "Not too sweet ya know?"

Lea looked around to see who he was talking to and not seeing anyone picked a box of Oreos grabbed a quart of milk and made her way to the front register. Jason was right behind her and as the cashier went to ring up her items Jason pushed his right up with hers.

Lea snapped right up.

"Excuse me sir those aren't mine," she said making it plain to the cashier that the groceries the man had pushed along with hers weren't hers. What nerve she thought. The few dollars she had came from the little babysitting job she had and the cookies and milk she was buying were putting a dent into that. Now this wanna be playa was trying to get slick and have her pay for his.

"You may think you're all that with your fly gear and all that bling but you've got the wrong sister this time," Lea said her head bobbing the way young girls do when they have an attitude.

"Whoa whoa sister. I wasn't expecting for you to pay for them. I was gonna take care of the bill. Only trying to be friendly is all." Jason said smiling. "Go ahead you can ring it up," he said nodding at the cashier before pulling out a wad of bills. Both Lea and the cashier who was not much older than Lea stared at the money. Jason chuckled to himself and flipped a twenty at the cashier.

"Will that cover everything," he asked.

The cashier still in awe of this young cat with all this money nodded before bagging the groceries. Jason picked up his groceries, before smiling at Lea and headed for the front door. Still stunned Lea didn't utter a word then realized that drug dealer or no drug dealer he was still due a thank you and hurried to the door to thank him before he drove off. Jason was climbing in the dark blue Lexus just as Lea stuck her head out the door and beckoned him. Pausing in his tracks Jason stood up acknowledging the petite seventeen year old.

"Yes ma'm."

"Just wanted to say thank you for picking up the tab," she said smiling now.

"Wow! That's a far cry from when you thought I was trying to scam you Miss Thang. It's not a problem though. By the way what's your name precious?"

"Lea."

"Well, it's certainly been a pleasure meeting you Lea. Mine's Jason. Jason Williams and I'm not trying to be fresh or anything but which way are you heading? I'd love to give you a lift, maybe talk and get to know you better," he said still grinning from ear-to-ear.

"Okay Jason. Jason Williams. Just because you paid for my groceries doesn't mean I'm getting in the car with your big money, drug dealing, wannabe a playa, ass." Lea's head was bobbing again and the hands on her hips tickled the young man.

"You sure are one hard chick," he said showing the perfect row of white teeth which contrasted nicely against his ebony skin.

"Why all the attitude though? You act like I killed your best friend."

"No but someone just like you did and my brother's in the middle of a six year bid for dealing with people just like you."

"And who are people like me." He asked. There was a more serious tone in his voice now.

"Drug dealers and hustlers," Lea replied angrily.

"Can I tell you something shorty?"

"Say what you want but I know your type with the flashy cars and stackin' papers and fly gear and how old are you? You can't be more than eighteen or nineteen at best. And you sure ain't making money like that at McDonalds or Wendys and that's the only jobs here in Raeford besides the turkey plant and even them that works there ain't stackin papers like that. Ain't nobody living like that but niggas out here dealin' in that poison. Trust. I may be young but I know what's out here in these streets."

"Goodness lady you don't even know me and you act like every young brotha out here wit' a lil' sumptin sumptin' gotta be slingin' and dealin' in dope or doin' sumptin' illegal."

"Most of 'em are."

"I ain't most baby and believe me I ain't never took no dope or sold no dope in my entire life," Offended at first by the girl's sudden onslaught, Jason was smiling once again.

"Where you live? My bad. Let me guess. You live in the Bottoms right?"

"You guessed right. But that ain't hard. Where else Black folks live in Raeford but the Bottoms?"

"I'm Black lived in Raeford my whole life and ain't never even been to the Bottoms baby. Hop in lady and let me show you some things you may not be aware of. Come on sweetheart. Jay ain't gonna do nothin' to harm you. Believe me I wouldn't jeopardize myself messin' with you. Life's too good and the future's too bright to let anything stupid get in the way," Jason said sliding into the front seat of the late model Lexus.

"So, let me get this right. Brotha can't be more than say twenty twenty-one at most, is pushing a new Lex, has a knot the size of my fist, pays for my stuff at the Seven Eleven and don't even know me and he's tryna tell me that he ain't slingin' something," Lea chuckled. " You can't be serious. Is that what you truly want me to believe? What that's saying' my mamas always throwin ' around something about I might be a newborn but I wasn't born yesterday," Lea said sliding in the car.

"Where to Mss Lady?"

"Names Lea not Miss Lady and I live in the Bottoms. Thought we already discussed that."

"The Bottoms it is then."

Jason turned up that new joint by J. Cole and eased into traffic. The two rode for a few minutes in silence accept for the sounds coming from the stereo and Lea had to admit she was impressed. He didn't play it so loud that everyone in the streets could hear it but only loud enough for the occupants of the car to bop their heads to the steady flow of the beat.

"You like J. Cole?"

"I really don't know artists names but I do like this song."

"You know he's from Fayetteville, right down the road apiece."

"I didn't know that. What you gonna tell me now? You his producer?" Lea said sitting up and taking notice of the car' direction. " And this is not the way to the Bottoms mister."

"I know I have to drop this cold medicine off to my dad. That's the real reason I was at the store and bumped into you. My dad's sick and asked me to run to the store and grab him something for his cold. Glad I did too. Gave me the chance to bump into you."

Lea watched, as the yards grew in size right along with the houses. She had heard about Adams Farm but had never had the occasion to visit and why would she have? She had a couple of White friends she attended school with but most of them lived right on the outskirts of the Bottoms and their parents worked at the only job in town and were only a little better off than her parents were. Still, she knew there was a segment of her high school where the kids had their own cars and drove to school. These were the affluent kids and it certainly wasn't often if ever that their paths crossed. She always wondered where they lived and now she knew were. The houses were gorgeous and Lea never having seen a mansion called them just that when in fact they merely middle and upper middle class working folks homes which fell in the hundred fifty, two hundred thousand dollar range. They were certainly nothing to sneeze at but neither were hey mansions. Jason pulled up in a long driveway that curved around and put the car in park.

"Come on in Lea. I'd like you to meet my mother and father. It's a good day it's Sunday and daddy's sick or else you'd never catch them both home at the same time," Jason said smiling.

Lea was even more leery than she was when she'd gotten in the car. Sure he seemed nice but he might be one of those serial rapists that set his victims up by buying their groceries at the local convenience store and then took them to some abandoned house where he raped them before dismembering them and boiling and eating their body parts. Lost in this thought and hesitant to open the car lea noticed a small dark skinned girl of about eight years of age who could have passed for Jason's twin running around her swing set in the backyard chased by an Irish setter nearly twice her size. Upon seeing Jason the little girl forgot the dog and headed straight for the boy screaming his name and leaping into his arms and screaming.

"Jason! Jason!"

"Hey Ann Marie," he said picking her up before tossing her another three feet in the air. He did this several times as she giggled with glee before putting her down.

"What did you buy me Jay," the tiny young girl said staring up at the young man the adoration beaming in her eyes.

"Do you think that every time I go to the store I have to buy you something?"

"Yep."

"And why do you think that?"

"Because Jay always says that Ann Marie is his favorite baby sister."

"And you know what? Ann Marie is absolutely right," Jason said sticking his hand in one of the bags and pulling out a pack of Twizzlers.

"The little girl squeezed her older brothers neck and thanked him before getting ready to run off but Jason grabbed her hand.

"I want you to meet somebody before you run off little lady."

"Lea this is my baby sister Ann Marie. Ann Marie this is my friend Lea..."

"Nice to meet you Ann Marie," Lea said almost sure it was safe to get out of the car now.

The little girl grabbed her older brothers pants leg and hid behind him with only her head peeking out and said hi.

"Is that your new girlfriend Jay?" She asked embarrassing both parties involved.

"Not yet, but maybe one day soon." He replied winking at his baby sister and not even bothering to look in Lea's direction.

Seemingly content with her older brother's answer the little girl let go of her brother's hand and went skipping off after the dog.

Jason held the door open for Lea.

A petite well-dressed brown skinned woman stood peeling an apple while a tall, distinguished, dark skinned man with a meticulously trimmed salt and pepper mustache stood staring at her with adoring eyes.

"Obama is like any other politician. He had me fooled at first with all his talk of change and hope. And because he was a Black man I thought he'd be more empathetic to our needs as Black people. Instead of working adamantly on Blacks and unemployment he's doing the same things the damn Republicans having been doing for the past fifty years."

"C'mon baby. That's not fair. You're looking for him to change in four short years what it took Bush eight years to mess up. He's a man. He ain't superman."

"Hell, yeah I'm expecting him to make good on all his campaign promises." she smiled. "You know we've always had to run twice as fast to get half as far. But instead of concentrating his efforts on the problems we're having right here at home he's at war in the Middle East and denying the Palestinians a homeland. It's a downright travesty especially when the real war is right here at home. What's he gonna do about that was lynched right here in Florida. Nothing that's what he's gonna do. Nothing! That could have very well been Jason," the woman said damn near screaming now.

The man could only smile. He loved the fact that his wife was so boisterous, so opinionated and so knowledgeable when it came to politics. It was one of the reasons he had been so attracted when they first met.

"I'm sorry honey. I didn't know you were home. Your father and I were just having one of spirited conversations on Obama is all. And who may I ask is this pretty young lady you've brought home?"

Jason turned and grabbed Lea by the hand.

"Lea these are my parents Mr. and Mrs. Hall. Mom, dad I'd like you to meet Lea."

"It's nice to meet you Lea. Are you a classmate of Jason's?"

"No ma'm. Actually, Jason and I just met."

"Oh, really? You must be quite special. It's rare that Jason brings a young lady home unless he really, really likes them," Mrs. Hall stated staring quizzically at her son.

"You're not helping my cause any mom," Jason said staring at the kitchen floor embarrassed that his mother had let the cat out the bag.

"Sorry son, I didn't mean to embarrass you. Why don't you give Lea a tour of the house?"

Glad to get away Jason grabbed Lea's hand for a second time. Lea was a little more at ease and smiling now as she followed Jason through the palatial home.

"I like your mom."

"Yeah, mom's a trip." Jason said quickly trying to change the subject. "And this is my room," he said proudly. Basketball trophies adorned three shelves and every empty space available in the room and a bookcase filled with every Black author Lea could think of. One shelf contained only Donald Goines books. Pulling out a couple and leafing through she said.

"You know my older brother used to read him and I never understood all the hullabaloo."

"You read a lot."

"Yes, I love to read. That's how I fill out my days. Whenever I have a little extra time that's what I do. Kills the time and the boredom and it helps me to travel without ever having to really move if you know what I'm saying."

"I do. I travel the same way," Jason laughed. He liked this girl and even though he'd just met her he felt some kinship to her that he rarely felt for other females. He didn't know why. He just did.

"Like when I read Donald Goines he takes me far away from here. He's real street and real grimy but when I read him I almost feel like I'm right there with him. And I ain't never been hood or ghetto despite your view of me."

"Well, unfortunately I've been in the Bottoms ever since I can remember but my dad always told me that you can be born and raised in the ghetto and you can be poor as dirt but you never have to be ghetto. And I believe that but I still like to read books on how the other half lives so I read a lot of things that are kind of out of the box I guess you'd say. You know not typical for an urban teenager."

"I hear you. I guess my parents would say the same things about me reading Goines," he laughed. "I guess you're always curious about things you don't know anything about."

"I guess."

"You ready for me take you home."

"I'm ready when you are."

"Don't say that. It's about lunchtime and if you say you're in no rush I'll do my best to keep you here all day."

They both laughed but Lea was in no rush. This was the first time in her seventeen years she had had the opportunity to rub noses with the rich and famous and she was curious. In another couple of years this is where she hoped to be.

"So tell me Jason…"

"Call me Jay. My friends all call me Jay."

"Okay, Jay tell me what is that allows you to drive a Lex at what eighteen or nineteen?"

Jason laughed immediately putting Lea back on the defensive.

"I'm sorry. I wasn't laughing at you. I just thought it was funny because Lord knows I couldn't afford that car without my parents. My dad wanted to upgrade about a year ago and when I graduated from high school and got a four year academic scholarship to go to college he was so proud of me and so happy that he wouldn't have to pay the thirty or so grand a year to go to Chapel Hill that he gave me the car as a graduation gift to say thank you."

"So you go to college?"

"Yeah, this is my first year at the University of North Carolina, Chapel Hill."

"What are you studying?"

"I'm going to become a pharmacist."

"You like it?"

"Yeah, I do. I mean so far I do. I just finished my first semester so yeah I guess I like it. My dad went to Chapel Hill so I kinda knew that's where he wanted me to go so I went but just between you and me I wish I had gone to someplace like Western Carolina or North Carolina Central."

"And why is that?"

"Well, I received four year basketball scholarships from both of them and I would have had a chance to play guard for both of them."

"And why can't you play ball at Chapel Hill?"

Jason started to laugh again but remembered her expression the last time he had and refrained.

"In honesty I don't know if I'm good enough. Chapel Hill is like the minor leagues for the NBA. Jordan and a lot of other great players came through there. They only want the top players in the country. They didn't recruit me so I'm not sure if I could make the grade. I've played with a few members of the

team and held my own but like I said they didn't recruit me so I don't know if I'm good enough but I certainly miss ball though. I've been playing for one team or another since I was like eight and this is the first I haven't had a chance to play organized ball. My dad told me to concentrate on the books and then see if they'll take me as a walk on this semester so that's what I'm gonna do. He hasn't steered me wrong yet so we'll see."

"So, what did your parents do to be able to afford such a beautiful home?

"Nothing out of the ordinary. My mom and dad both teach at Fayetteville State."

"They're college professors? Wow that's my dream. I want to be an English professor."

"And what's to stop you?"

"Nothing. It just seems so far away."

"But it's not. One day it seems like that and the next day it's all behind you."

"Listen to you sounding like an old man looking back at his life," Lea laughed. "You can't be more than a year or two older than I am. How old are you anyway Jay?"

Jason had to smile too. He hadn't meant to come off like that.

"I just turned nineteen," he said laughing. "Come on Lea. Mom probably already has lunch on the table and she gets evil when she's prepared something and we're not there when she puts it out."

"Does she know you invited me to lunch? I don't want to seem pushy or imposing."

"You don't know my mother," Jason laughed before grabbing Lea's hand and taking her down the long and winding stairs and back to the kitchen. There were five plates of food set out on the table and no sooner than they arrived in the kitchen Mrs. Hall had Lea by the elbow and was guiding her to her seat. Jason could only smile. Mom would never change that he was sure of.

"I didn't know if you liked tomatoes so you'll notice there off to the side. There's lemonade and iced tea out as well. I didn't want to take the liberties of pouring you something that you aren't to fond of so I just put them both out. You can take your pick."

"Whichever you would have poured would have been fine Mrs. Hall. Thank you so much. It looks awfully good."

"I like her Jason. I think you may have a keeper this time," his mother said referring to Lea.

Lea smiled graciously before digging. She hadn't realized just how hungry she was and the food was tasty to say the least. Only once did she look up to see if anyone was paying any attention to what a voracious appetite she had but everyone seemed as hungry as she was and so once again she settled in. When she was finished she thanked Mrs. Hall again before following Jason out to the pool where they sat and talked and got to know each other until far into the evening.

When Lea woke up the next morning her only thoughts were of the polite, young man she'd the previous day with. When he dropped her off she joked about him being a perfect gentleman the entire day and she hoped he wouldn't push up on her now and ask or try to steal a kiss. He'd responded by saying that he was hoping the same thing but when that time did arise she would be the one pushing up. Lea smiled at the thought. He certainly was cocky and self-assured. But then why wouldn't he be? He had the world by the throat. With his good looks, money, and his life all planned out he was the one in demand and a girl would be a fool not to scoop him up the first chance she had.

They'd exchanged numbers and just because he occupied her every thought that Saturday morning she refused to pick up her phone and call him. Yet, every time the phone rang she'd rush to it hoping that it was him. It was like this all morning and most of the afternoon. By the time evening had arrived Lea was literally spent from anxiety and he still hadn't called. Maybe she was like one of those Donald Goines books he was so fond of. Maybe she was just an experiment to see how a girl from the Bottoms was. The more she thought the more it bothered her and then the phone rang.

"Hello may I speak to Lea?"

"This is she."

"Lea this is Jay. Damn girl I don't know what you did to me but you've been on my mind all day."

"I guess that's why you called me this morning."

"I wanted to but my dad had me working all day. It's almost as if he knew I had plans and wasn't having any parts of it," Jay laughed. "But on the real, what did you do to me. All I've been wanting to do is spend some more time with you."

Lea smiled but decided to play it cool and let him sweat and refused to tell him she'd been feeling the same way. She had to admit Jason was extremely nice guy and seemed to be upfront and open and honest about his feelings. He was certainly far from these thugs she was accustomed to down in the bottoms. They were all so hard and afraid to show their true feelings because someone might suspect them of not being hard and Lord knows nobody wanted to be thought of as a punk down in the Bottoms. That was like being fresh meat in the joint. No, down here the common feeling was M-O-B—money over bitches. Getting paid was important women weren't. They could like everything else be bought and sold. And you never ever let a woman get close because their aim was to steal your heart

and once they did that they had the ability to pimp a nigga as well as any pimp could pimp a woman. But Jason was different. He hadn't grown up with that ghetto mentality of getting him before he gets you and neither had she even though she was cautious in exposing her feelings.

Lea listened and when he finished explaining and asked if she would like to go to the movies at ten she took her time in answering. There was no movie theatre in Raeford. The closest one was in Fayetteville and she had only been there once in her seventeen years. It wasn't like she missed it. She just hadn't been but she jumped at the chance to go now. He had mentioned the name of the movie but she hadn't paid any attention. It could have been 'All Dogs Go To Heaven' for all she cared.

The bottom line is she liked him enough to want to spend time with him. He was so different, so unlike any of the boys she knew and talked to. He was like those books she read and traveled vicariously with. He had opened doors and made her curious about a number of things and not only had he made her curious he was patient and content with answering the questions she was so curious about and she liked that.

It was seven o'clock when he'd phoned and though her closet was sparse to say the least she began preparing her outfit right then and there. After going through the few clothes she had Lea became disgusted and sat on her bed and cried. She'd never really been concerned with keeping up with the other kids in school after all she was from the Bottoms and almost everyone that lived there was in the same predicament. Her parents like most of the folks that lived there were employed by the only industry in town—the turkey plant and as everyone knew the House of Raeford didn't pay very well. But she had never really been aware of just how poor she was. When everyone around you was in the same boat it was more or less the norm. But after visiting the Hall's she suddenly became aware of just how poor she was. And as she tried to put an outfit together she realized just what being poor really meant. She'd tried to get a job at the three fast food joints in town but then so were the rest of the Black kids in the Bottoms and there just weren't that many opportunities available. Babysitting was cool but she just didn't get that many calls or that many hours and it was only good for lunch money and a snack or two on the way home from school. Still, she hadn't felt the full effect of her being poor until tonight.

After crying for what seemed like hours and deciding not to go Lea finally decided on a pair of black jeans that the color had faded from from being washed too many times. Finding them she threw them in the washing machine and rushed down to the coin laundry to dry them before rushing home and ironing them. She tried to iron the newness back into them. When she'd finished she had creases sharp enough to draw blood. Satisfied she took a black wool sweater out of her top dresser drawer, picked the lint balls off of it and pulled it over her head.

The tears were still welling up in Lea's eye when Mrs. Hudson walked into her daughter's bedroom. She couldn't believe her daughter had been crying. Of her three children she had always been the strongest and showed the most promise in her mother's eyes. Her oldest son had like many of the young Black men in the Bottoms gotten caught up in the drug game at first selling and eventually using and was now in the second year of a six-year bid. Then there was the middle girl who fell in love with her six-grade

boyfriend. She now had four children, each a year apart and was pregnant with the fifth. She'd never wanted to do anything but get married and have kids and that's exactly what she was doing. Well, ecept for the marrying part…

But Lea was different. A good student, her teachers would always applaud her efforts and commend her mother for the fine job she'd done with Lea, which always made Mrs. Hunter feel proud. More than that Mrs. Hunter never had to fear that Lea would get caught up in all the harmful goings on that took place in the Bottoms. No, one thing that she never had to worry about was Lea succumbing to the bullshit that made life so difficult in the ghetto.

There were only two times she'd ever seen Lea cry and that was when her daddy left her when she was seven years old. She'd cried for about a week then. The second time was when Chris had been killed. And tonight. Mrs. Hunter was more surpised than anything.

"What's wrong Lea," she asked the pain and concern showing brightly in her eyes. "I thought you had a date with Mr. Wonderful tonight."

The tears flowed freely as soon as her mother finished the sentence.

"What did I say?" Her mother asked now feeling responsible for her daughter's tears.

"It's nothing mommy." Lea said brushing the tears from her eyes and trying to regain her composure.

"It must be something. Nobody cries for just nothing and especially you Lea. You've always been like the Rock of Gibraltar. And here you are crying your eyes out and telling me that nothing's wrong."

"It's okay mommy. I was just having a little pity party is all. Was getting ready to go out tonight and realized I don't have any clothes. It never dawned on me that we were poor until I went to Jason's house and saw how other people live. Other Black people mama. And I know he's going to be all dressed up to take me out and I looked in my drawer. Mama, I have two pairs of jeans and three sweaters. That's it. And I'm trying to date this rich, college guy and my poor ghetto behind just ain't seeing it happening."

"Oh my God girl I know you're not serious. If that boy truly likes you it doesn't matter what you have on. He asked you out Lea because he likes you not the clothes you wear. If it were all about the clothes he could just hang out in Macy's and push up on one of them well dressed mannequins."

Lea smiled at her mother's silliness.

"But on the real mommy, after this I probably won't see him again," she said her eyes welling up with tears again.

"Your grandmother used to always say, 'take one day at a time. You never know what tomorrow may bring."

"Yeah, like I might hit the lottery."

"Stop the nonsense and get dressed Lea. Don't keep that young man waiting over something as trivial as this."

Jason sat in the living room and came to his feet when Lea entered the room and smiled broadly.

"Hey lady. Wow, you look even better than you did when I left you."

Lea was glad he approved.

"But I don't know who looks younger—you or your mom."

Mrs. Hunter smiled appreciatively.

"This young man really knows how to charm a woman. You two get out of here and please don't have my baby out too late young man."

"I'll have her home before the clock strikes twelve ma'm."

"That'll be fine."

It had been years since Lea had been to the movies. She could remember her dad taking her to see the Lion King but that was years ago.

Jason took her to see Planet of the Apes and it was alright although this new one hardly rated with the reruns she'd seen of the old Plant of the Apes. But it didn't much matter to her at the time. Just being with him made the evening exciting she thought as she rested her head on his shoulder. He was watching the movie and at intervals muttered this and that to her concerning the movie while she watched just enough to be able to respond intelligently. When the movie was over the two walked in the now closed mall until they reached the exit where Jason held the door then grabbed her arm and kissed her gently. She responded accepting his kiss anxiously. She felt a warm glow all over as his tongue found her mouth and she knew immediately that she was his for the taking. Lea had never had a boyfriend. The closest she'd ever come to having one was Chris but he'd been killed before anything had really taken place. Lea had never felt quite so good before. Whoever said that love was grand sure wasn't lying. Jason drove back to Raeford so slowly Lea had to tell him he was going to get a ticket for doing the minimum speed limit. But Jason figured the slower he drove the more time he could spend with Lea and so a minute or two after he picked up the speed he slowed it down again.

"So have you made plans on where you want to go to school next year Lea?"

"I haven't really thought about it. I mean it isn't as if I've been blowing it off. I've applied to about twenty or twenty-five colleges. All the money I get goes into application fees but I haven't really gotten my hopes up over any particular college. I'm trying to follow in your footsteps oh great one."

"How's that?"

"I'm trying to get a four year academic scholarship and the first and best school; to give me one is where I'll be going. That's why I'm not picking any one particular school and setting my sights on it."

"I hear you. Did you apply to UNC?"

"Yeah, but I haven't heard anything from them yet."

"Do you know what you're going to major in?"

"Have no clue? What's yours?"

"You."

"No, what I'm asking you is if you've declared a major yet."

"And I answered."

"No silly. I'm serious?"

"I am too. I want to study you," Jason said smiling. "Only I'm not sure four years will be enough time to allow me to get to adequately know you."

"You're cute Jason," Lea said smiling.

"Glad you think so. I feel the same way about you sweetie."

"But seriously Jay what are you majoring in? I'm curious. I don't have long and I'll have to declare one as well and I don't have a clue. Thought you maybe able to offer a little encouragement and advice."

"That you'll have to decide on your own and I know it doesn't seem like you have that long but trust I'll walk you through it and it'll be fine. Would you like to ride down to Carolina before my breaks over? I think you'll like it. The campus is really nice and Franklin St. is the stuff. But tonight all I want to do is talk about you and me. You know—us."

"What about us?"

"I was wondering, more like hoping that I could somehow keep you?"

Lea laughed.

"You want to keep me like what like old baseball cards?"

"See why are you always making light when I'm trying to be serious?"

Lea wiped the smile from her face.

"I wasn't actually making fun of you Jay. It's just the way you phrase everything. Why can't you just come out and say things that you want to say without all the ambiguity?"

"Cause the ambiguity and intrigue are what makes it special. I like the cat and mouse game, the chase, the intrigue. That's what turns me on. It's one thing to say you want dessert. It's totally different when you say you want the chocolate mousse. I like to see and envision and plan what I'm going to have. I want to take it slow and strategize. Want to take my time and lay the bait. And then lure my prey in. I don't want to just walk into the local Giant Eagle or Food Lion and grab a piece of meat. You feel me?"

"In that case, it wouldn't be right for me to just concede to your requests to keep me. You need your prey to be elusive so that you can enjoy the chase."

Jason laughed.

"Play it anyway you want but I intend on making you mine before it's over that I will tell say."

"Is that right?"

"Trust."

"This should be interesting?" Was all Lea could manage to muster.

The rest of the ride was cordial, each feeling the other out like two chess players vying for position, waiting for the other to make a miscue so they could take the advantage and eventually grab the upper hand and win the match. But with Jay and Lea there were no losers. They both could and would win and they both knew that. For the next several weeks they both did everything within reason to make the other happy and Mrs. Hunter had to admit that she had never seen her daughter happier. When Thanksgiving break finally came to an end and it was time for Jason to return to Chapel Hill he did so with little or no interest and even contemplated transferring to UNC Pembroke which was only one country hick town a few miles away in Lumberton. A branch it hardly held the same prestige of the older and much more heralded campus. Still, it had been a thought. After ruling that out and after attempting to commute the hour and a half long drive everyday Jason eventually fell into the daily ritual of school and resigned himself to seeing Lea at the Christmas break Lea, on the other hand, decided on attending Chapel Hill and upon receiving the acceptance letter she steadied herself and relegated herself to the fact that there was no need to rush anything but only bide her time and they would eventually together again. Still, there was the here and now and neither wanted to waste the time they had to spend together.

During their time apart Lea now spent her every waking hour preparing for their reunion. On one of his visits home Jason mentioned moving off campus and getting an apartment for the two of them. Lea welcomed the idea and the idea of sharing an apartment with Jay consumed her every waking thought. There were no more movies or eating out now. Instead the time they spent together was spent browsing and shopping at Pier 1 and buying knick-knacks for their apartment. Lea was ecstatic and Jay was his normal charming self, letting Lea pick out everything while he played the part of the good husband standing idly by as she oohed and ahhed over table settings and bed spreads.

And at the end he'd swipe his debit card and grab the armload of bags and head to the car. Jason couldn't remember ever having been so in love. When Lea would offer to make a contribution he would always turn her down and at first it had been okay but more and more it began to bother her.

The days went on as usual with her attending school and applying herself as if her very life depended on it even though she had already been accepted and was already there except for the formality of finishing high school. She was going to begin in the summer so as to knock off her first semester and get a jump on the entering college freshman. And thus get through the initial indoctrination and enable herself to be able to take an overload of credits by the time the other freshman were just getting their feet wet. This was her plan and everyone thought it a good one except Mrs. Hunter who wondered if this wouldn't be a lot of pressure on her daughter who despite her common sense and energy had never really encountered the demands of the real world.

Still, the old woman kept her thoughts to herself. Out of her three children, Lea was the one who had made the best choices when it came to her life and since things had always worked out and Lea had never done anything but make her mother proud of her Mrs. Hudson held her tongue when Lea informed her of her plans. Besides the older woman knew that in seventeen years she'd done basically all she could do and now Lea would have to make her own decisions and mistakes but there was little she could do when it came to guiding her daughter. It was time to cut the apron strings.

And for the most part things continued as they always had. Lea had always been a loner but now it seemed that Lea was beginning to venture out just a little bit more. Jason became a regular visitor and when not at Chapel he was there with Lea and Mrs. Hudson. There were days when Lea was in school when Jason would sit with Mrs. Hudson and be content to do the chores Mrs. Hudson was now unable to do like the yard work, or repair the fence and other things around the house that needed mending. When he wasn't tending to the old woman's needs he'd come over, spread his homework over the dining room table and work on some paper or other school assignment. There were times, long after Lea had fallen asleep when Mrs. Hudson brought him a blanket and wrapped it around his shoulders and led him to the living room couch where he would sleep the night through. She liked Jason and only

wished he could have been her own child. He was certainly a good influence on Lea at a point in Lea's life when she really needed some positive guidance and could lead her in her ways Mrs. Husband couldn't. Having only a sixth grade education she was in unchartered waters now when it came to Lea's college preparations. But even with Jason there when he could be Mrs. Hunter was beginning to notice a change in her daughter but could only attribute it to her growing up but still she felt a little fearful, perhaps a little apprehensive about her daughter's changing behavior. Even Jason noticed the change.

On several occasions he'd stopped by to see Lea and although he'd made his way his way over to see she and Mrs. Hudson there was no question who he'd come to see. They'd sit and chat for a while but Carrie or Ebony would knock at the door and Lea would tell both Jason and her mother that she'd be back soon. At first her mother addressed her.

"May I speak to young lady."

"Yeah ma. What's up?"

"In the kitchen young lady." Lea knew from the tone of her mother's voice that the older woman was angry but where there was a time when Lea would have gone to the ends of the earth not to see her mother upset nowadays it didn't seem to matter much whether the elderly woman was upset or not. Nowadays Lea had her own agenda and neither Jason nor her mother seemed either privy to it or welcomed to share it.

Lea leaned against the refrigerator door while her mother excused herself from Lea's visitors.

"Lea. What in the hell are you doing? Jason's been here since one o'clock this afternoon. You come in from school, talk to him for a hot minute when Ebony and that other little hussy comes in and you act like that young man isn't even here. How the hell are you going to get up and leave your company? I know I've brought you up better than that. That boy ain't coming to see me. He's coming to see you and you're just being rude and that is not the Lea that I raised."

"Look mommy I didn't ask him to stop by. This is my senior year and I'm supposed to be able to let my hair down a little. But every time I look up he's here."

"Then that's what you tell him but don't be rude about it. It's not my job to entertain your male friends and it is certainly no daughter of mine that gets up and leaves her company for me to entertain when they came to see you. You're almost eighteen years old and headed off to be on your own. Mommy ain't gonna be around to handle your dirty work then and I sure as shit ain't doing it now. Now you march right on in there and handle your business. And tell me something else young lady while we're on the subject. Isn't that the little heifer who only a year or so ago you told me you wouldn't be caught dead around."

"People change mommy," Lea said dropping her eyes to the floor to avoid the angry glare of her mother's eyes. From the tone of her mother's voice she knew the woman was angry. It was something Lea seldom saw and never but never was her mother's anger exacted towards her.

"I don't know about people changing but you certainly have. I'm surprised at you Lea. Now go in there and tell that boy that you don't want him around if you don't want him around then you get them two little heifers out of my house before I chase them the hell out."

Excusing herself as she brushed passed her mother, Lea walked into the living room only to find Jason gone.

"Cutie pie wants you to give him a call," Carrie said smiling at Lea.

"Good thing you're my girl Lea or I'd have that nigga screamin' my name all night long," Ebony continued. "Damn, if that boy ain't got a sweet ass on him. What I could do with that shit," she said smiling and talking to no one in particular.

"Fuck that ass. Did you see that chain and that watch? And let's not forget the car. I can see why you tryna step yo game up and tryna get paid now."

"Say goodnight ladies and I do use the word ladies loosely," Mrs. Hudson said as she stood in the living room doorway listening.

"Night Mrs. Hudson."

"Night ma'am."

"I won't be home too late mommy."

"I certainly hope not. You know tomorrow's a school day."

"I know mommy. I have my key so don't wait up," Lea said closing the front door behind her.

"Damn Lea. I got to give it to you. The brother is fine. And you gonna tell me he ain't slingin' or nothing?"

"No. He just works and goes to school full time. That's it."

"Then he must be workin' his shit on the side. I once knew this brother that used to be called Night that was like your boy Jay. He was about twenty and real fine. I'm talking Denzel fine who used to pimp himself at night for all these old forty and fifty year old bitches and my boy used to clean up. Them old bitches used to love them some Night and he used to feed their fantasies and do all the things their husbands wouldn't or couldn't do. You sure your boy ain't pimpin' himself?"

"No. Jay's parents are both college professors at Fayetteville State and he's their only son so they spoil him is all."

"Real talk?" Ebony said amazed. "I ain't never seen no rich niggas 'cept on TV. You go Lea. You done really hit the jackpot this time. I'm happy for you. I guess I can understand why you feel the need to make some cheddar with the quickness now. When you runnin' wit' the big dogs you've got to really step yo game up."

"Can't be a Bottoms girl all yo life," Carrie added. "Shit, sometimes you gotta do what you gotta do just to elevate yourself outta the hell hole you born into. Ain't that right E.?"

"You ain't neva said it betta," Ebony said giving Carrie a high five.

Both girls were seniors and the talk of Raeford Senior High School. Both were attractive but dressed and acted much older than their years and were the envy of most of the Bottoms girls. They dressed nicer, hung out with men with money and never ever could you tell that they lacked for anything. Some students had them pegged as runway models while others depicted them as video hos but one thing no one could say was that was that they were typical Bottoms girls. Lea, who hadn't been exposed to much outside the Bottoms, also recognized the distinction between the two and most of the other girls who resembled her in their poverty. And although she didn't know how or what they did to be so different she was certainly going to find out. In less than six months she would be entering a different world, Jason's world. A world which she was becoming all too familiar with and a world she yearned to be a part of. The trips that now were all too frequent down to Chapel Hill revealed Black kids her age that were so much alike her and yet so different but the only difference she could see was that of money and she was intent on evening up the odds no matter what it took.

In time, she'd even discussed the differences and discrepancies with Jason but he'd only laughed and made the comment that he'd choose her over ninety per cent of the Black girls on campus just because she was real and genuine but she knew he was just saying that because that's who he was and he didn't want to hurt her feelings. But deep down inside she knew that the first fly hottie that came from New York to attend school there in all their fly gear, talking that hip thing with her pink Tims and Evisu jeans and he'd be history. No, she had to do what she had to do and at least put herself in contention, in the

running and so here she was sidelining Jay for a minute or two and evening up the odds in an attempt at making the playing field a little more level.

"You sure you want to do this Lea. I mean out of all the girls at school you'd be the last one I'd expect to put yourself out there like this. I mean I don't know about Carrie but I didn't have a choice. There was eleven of us all under one roof and just momma to provide for all of us so I didn't have much of a choice. But for you it ain't that crucial and I'm gonna tell you—and this is real talk—once you go through with this Lea there ain't no turning back and I swear to you on my mother's life things will never be the same."

"Shut the hell up Ebony. Look at the burden you've taken off your mother. Your little brothers and sisters are eating and don't want for hardly nothing. Plus all the girls in the Bottoms give you much respect cause you handlin' your business better than most grown folks twice your age."

"All that may be true but I'd give it all up if I had the chance to do it all over again. I'm serious. Fuck the money. I'd give it all up just to be where Lea is right now. I know you like this guy Lea but if he can't accept you as you are then the hell with him. But from what I can see what's his name will take you any way he can get you. He ain't thinking about the clothes or how much dough you got. He just likes you for you but you got in your mind that you got to step your game up just to be with him. And if that's what it is then I can help you out with some clothes and a little change here and there to get you over. It sure would be nice to see someone get out of the Bottoms and make something out of themselves, ya know what I'm sayin'? I mean the decision is all yours but on the real I think what you're about to do is a mistake Lea. Take it from someone who's been there and livin' the lie."

"Leave her alone and let the girl get paid. She's gonna need some cheddar to hang with Mr. Wonderful. They getting ready to set up shop and her po' ass ain't got shit to bring to the table," Carrie said lighting a Newport.

"Shut the fuck up Carrie. Lea's got a future and you know it but you're a typical hater. You're a typical lowlife, bottom feedin' nigga. You're a fuckin' crab and instead of tryin' to help someone move in the right direction you gonna try to hold them down cause you ain't got no future and ain't going nowhere your damn self. You know damn well that Lea's got too much going for her than to be out here in these streets with the likes of these sheisty, no-good pedifiles."

"Whatever!" was all Carrie could manage.

Lea, who had been listening intently, was even more unsure than she'd been at the outset and she'd had reservations then. Still, she walked keeping pace with the other two girls until they came to a large white house with black shutters. The yard was meticulously kept with petunias and azaleas strategically placed and only one light shone through the kitchen windows.

Lea was at once apprehensive as Carrie unlatched the front gate lock and entered and made her way up the narrow walkway followed by Ebony and Lea. Tapping lightly she pushed the front door open and entered what appeared to be a foyer. On the right was a small parlor or sitting room and Ebony, obviously familiar with her surroundings went in and had a seat. Lea and Carrie followed and sat in the well-furnished Queen Anne chairs. Here they remained for several minutes until a dark-skinned elderly woman entered. The woman appeared to be in her late fifties, early sixties and was elegantly attired in a silver and black sequined gown that looked to have cost in the neighborhood of a few grand at least.

"Miss Lena, I'd like for you to meet my good friend Lea," Ebony said. "You already know Carrie," she said as an afterthought.

Both girls paid homage to the older woman who was obviously the matriarch of the old, and spacious, Victorian home.

"Is there something I can do for you Ebony?"

"Yes, Ms. Lena. Do you mind if I speak to you in private?"

"Sure, Ebony. Step right this way. Is there anything I can get you ladies? A glass of wine, a cold soda…"

"A glass of wine would be fine Ms. Lena," Carrie said.

"Wine would be fine, thank you." Lea said when the older woman glanced her way.

"I'll send someone in with your wine, she said before turning and sashaying away. Ms. Lena was a fairly large brown skinned woman with hips, ass, and breasts protruding just enough to make a man even at her age turn and take notice. And take notice they did. With her street savvy, God given talents, and wit that both men and women adored Ms. Lena owned her own brothel by the age of twenty-three and by the age of thirty had a string of brothels which ran from Boston to Miami. She had long since retired and moved back to her hometown of Raeford and kept this one open just for the sake of having something to do in her retirement. And this establishment, a retirement of sorts for Miss Lena was run in the same manner with the same strict rules she'd run her others.

There was no hard liquor served on the premises. She served wine and only the best wine at that. That way she kept control of things and kept the madness to a minimum. Just to assure safety and security for her young ladies she kept two huge bouncers and required that they work out at least three times a week to maintain the physical prowess needed to intimidate wanna be thugs, gangstas and anyone who thought they could gain entry intoxicated. She paid off the local police once a month like clockwork always on the same day at the same time and any of her girls found in trouble with the law or suspected of using an illegal substance was immediately let go. After all, girls in need of employment were a dime

a dozen in Raeford. This is how Ms. Lena ran a clean joint and maintained order and Ebony was one of her best earners. Both women had a great amount of respect for the other and if Ms. Lena had a heir apparent and was grooming anyone everyone recognized that it would be Ebony.

"Hey Ms. Lena I brought you a young lady who says she wants to try working."

"And what do you think?"

"Well, when she first approached me I was all for it. I thought she was a typical Bottoms bitch like Carrie—ya know—with no purpose, no direction—that just wanted to make some quick money so she could hang out in one of the local dives and drink or drug herself to death when this shit finally caught up with her. But the more I got to know her the more I can see that she's different than all the rest of the girls."

"How do you know her?"

"I go to school with her."

"And how is she doing in school?"

"That's what I'm trying to tell you Ms. Lena. The girl is in the top five in the senior class. She just received a four year academic scholarship to the University of North Carolina. I wish I had a four year academic scholarship to go anywhere but she got one to the second best college in North Carolina and she wants to throw it all away because she met this guy whose parents have a little bit of money who goes there. They plan on getting an apartment together and since she can't roll with him financially she wants to try hooking."

"And what do you think?"

"I think she's throwing away her future if you want my honest answer."

"Did you tell her this?"

"Yeah I told her just what I'm telling you but she's got Carrie in her ear telling her all this shit about how she won't be able to keep her man if she ain't got no dough and how good it feels to have money and nice clothes all the time."

"And what does she think?"

"Well, if you ask me she's not really sure. That's why I'm telling you. Maybe you can talk some sense into her."

"Is that what you want me to do Ebony?"

"Yes mam. That's what I want you to do."

"Well, she is a cute little thing and would make a welcome addition to my stable but if that's what you want me to do then I'll try. I don't know if I'll have any better luck than you did but I'll give it a try. If I don't have any luck convincing her she can go to room fourteen and I'll set her up with two of my older, more reliable customers and she'll get a minimum of two hundred dollars per customer. Do you know if she's had sex before?"

"I don't know but I sincerely doubt it. Why?"

"If she's a virgin then that in itself is a selling point and can almost double her value. Old white men are crazy about young Black virgins."

"Oh hell no. Please talk to her Ms. Lena. That ain't no way to have your first sexual encounter."

The older woman laughed.

"You're right but whose decision is that for you and I to make," and with that she got up from behind her desk, ground her cigarette out in the gold rimmed ashtray in front of her and headed for the parlor.

"Meanwhile, you can take the john in room sixteen. Carrie's already up there. He wants the double team and she's already started. Don't worry about your girl. Either way it goes I'll take good care of her."

"Thanks Ms. Lena."

"Anytime, Ebony. Send Lea in on your way up would you please?"

Lea walked into Ms. Lena's office and was surprised to find how tastefully decorated it was. A huge mahogany desk sat on a rich brown oriental rug. A mahogany bookcase stood in one corner of the office full of books. Lea glanced over and recognized quite a few of the authors most of whom were Black. Ms. Lena watched the young lady closely.

She made her living in large part by doing just this and had a keen sense of people their dreams, desires and often times their fetishes.

"You like to read?" Ms. Lena inquired trying to get a feel for this young girl who sat in front of her. Lea's face perked up.

"I love to read and I like your taste in authors. I see you have Zora Neal and Langston Hughes. They're two of my very favorites but I don't believe I've ever read As I Wander by Hughes."

Ms. Lena smiled. She'd come across a lot of young girls in her time but none quite so bright and articulate as the one who now sat before her.

"Ebony tells me that you want to make some extra money."

"That I do," Lea answered crossing her leg and letting the split on her dress fall gracefully to the side.

"And that you can do. Not only can you make a good deal in this trade and you can make a great deal in a relatively short amount of time. Let's see. It's almost eight-thirty now. If I were to send you upstairs now I could almost guarantee you four or five hundred dollars by midnight."

Ms. Lena watched as the young girls grew to be almost the size of quarters.

"That's the upside. But wherever there's an upside to something there's always a downside. And it wouldn't be fair if I didn't tell you the downside."

Ms. Lena picked up the tiny bell on her desk and shook it twice. A second or two a tall dark skinned woman with a shape that most men would die for entered the office and said, "Yes, ma'm." To which Ms. Lena said "Jasmine would you please get me a glass of sherry and my young friend here a glass of Zinfandel."

Jasmine smiled and the worn face with the wrinkles and crow's feet spoke of the woman having seen better days.

When Jasmine was no longer in view Lena turned and looked at Lea.

"That was one of my top girls, one of my top money earners. She's been known to pull in close to fifteen hundred a night and that was only a couple of years ago. Jasmine used to be at the top of every man's wish list. Now she's reduced to serving drinks for a couple of hundred dollars a weeks plus tips."

Jasmine soon returned and handed Ms. Lena and Lea their drinks.

"Can I ask you for one more small favor Jasmine?"

"Sure, Lena."

"I want you to grab yourself a drink and pull up a chair."

The middle-aged woman returned to the room and pulled up a chair alongside of Lea.

"First of all, I want you to tell this young lady how old you are Jasmine."

Jasmine smiled knowing exactly where the conversation was headed.

"On Sunday I'll be twenty-three."

Lea tried to hide the shock that filled her face but when Jasmine read the young girl's face she knew exactly what she was thinking. Lea had

Jasmine pegged for at least forty-five maybe fifty but no way twenty-three.

"Jasmine's been with me since she was sixteen. What's that? Seven years..."

"Yeah, I was just about your age when I started. I was full of fire and brimstone, ready to rip and run. I thought the world was mine. I was making money hand over fist—I mean crazy money. Life was good and then before you know it when most young girls are just started to hit their prime and finishing up college and just getting ready to start their lives and their careers I looked up and mine is over and I wish it were that simple. I contracted AIDS when I was nineteen and have been living with it or dying from it for the last four years and all because I wanted or thought I wanted to live the fast life when I was just a kid. It's funny but I wish I had someone to sit me down and tell me all the pros and cons of it but nobody cared about anything except how much my pretty ass could pull in a night. Now no one outside of Ms. Lena gives a fuck. So, if you're even considering giving this thing a twirl you best damn sure know what you're getting into. This here is the safest house in the world. Ms. Lena don't let no riff raff in and keeps the drama down to a minimum. She makes sure all her girls are clean and get cleared before we can take on any customers and then makes it a requirement that we get a doctor's clearance every six months. That's to protect the customers but there ain't shit to protect us from them and just like this motherfucker give me something they can sho'nuff give it to you."

"Thank you Jasmine."

"No problem. You have any questions Lea. Ask now. Don' just jump into something before you research it thoroughly and trust girlfriend I'm speaking from experience. And as you can see experience isn't always the best teacher."

"Yes ma'm," Lea replied almost whispering now.

"Thanks again, Jasmine," Ms. Lena repeated.

"Like I said—not a problem if I can keep a pretty young thang like that from fucking up her life like I did mine," she said closing the door behind her.

"Jasmine's always been one of my favorites. It's a damn shame though. I've always been a firm believer though that if you keep rolling the dice your number will eventually come up. And Jasmine was rolling the dice faster than any girl I've ever seen and I guess the law of averages finally caught up with her and her number just came up. It's sad but this isn't a game and if you're not careful and even if you are there's a good chance that you won't survive."

The woman looked at Lea and was deadpanned in her stare. She did her best to assess the girl's thoughts and knew that if this child had any kind of sense of self, any self-esteem, and any sense she'd pull up stakes before she planted any and run like hell. Always a good judge of character she threw in the clincher.

"Ebony tells me you're involved with a rather intelligent young man who's received a four year academic scholarship to Carolina. Says you've received one too and you start this upcoming semester."

"Yes, mam."

"She also tells me that you're a little short on money and that's why you're considering being a working girl."

"Yes mam."

"In that case, I have a proposition for you Lea. But it's solely up to you and I'm praying you use your good judgment after what Jasmine and Ebony have told you. Now here's my proposition. You can go upstairs in room fourteen and entertain two or three guests and leave work with four or five hundred dollars or I can put some money towards you starting school at Carolina. I'll give you two thousand dollars at the beginning of the school year and every semester you make the dean's list. To be honest you could make that same two thousand in less than a week's time but that's the decision you'll have to make. I can tell you this though. Your boyfriend and no other man will want to make you his girlfriend or his wife once they find out that you whore for a living. And trust me they will find out. They always do. The smell of prostitution sort of lingers around you and no matter how much you wash you can't get the smell to go away. You will reek of it. Make your decision dear. Ms. Lena has work to do."

A month later, Lea sat in the passenger side of Jason's Lexus smiling and giggling and enjoying the sounds of Jay Z's new album. She couldn't wait to begin her first semester not dressed in the latest fashions but draped in Carolina blue.

Ball Don't Lie

The stands erupted as he went high to pull down yet another rebound. He wasn't sure how many he had up to that point but he knew it had to be in the neighborhood of twenty or so. Coach had asked him to change his focus from the offensive end to the defensive end and concentrate on defense and rebounding so he could initiate the break and so far he'd done just that.

This was a team they were just naturally supposed to beat. The Blue Devils were coming into the season after having lost three starters, all seniors, and their highly recruited freshman had a torn ACL and was out for the season. And with a make shift team with three walk-ons they'd still somehow managed to keep it close and make it a game. With two minutes left in the fourth Jackson held on to a rather tenuous one point lead.

Still, it didn't matter who was on the roster for Jackson he knew that this would be a hard fought battle, probably the toughest game of the year, (at least for him). And this was one game he never had a problem getting up for. All the kids from Jackson were his friends and lived in his neighborhood. It was a rough school, one of the worst in the city and when it came time for him to attend moms had objected and everyone who knew Mrs. Ali knew that when the tiny little woman made up her mind there was no need to object and so each and every day for the past three years Malik had to get up at six am and start the long, arduous hour and a half trek to Immaculate Conception, the little all White school out in the lily White suburbs of Jersey.

All his classmates were White and at first this bothered him but as soon as he entered the gym everything felt normal and those very same kids who had looked at him out of the corners of their eyes were suddenly making small talk and inviting them to their little after school functions and parties on the weekend. The word had gotten around about his basketball prowess and for the first time in years it looked like the school would be a legitimate contender for the city championship.

At six seven and a lithe one hundred and ninety pounds Malik Ali better known as Bliss had all the gifts to go to the NBA straight from high school and pro scouts had started visiting him as early as his sophomore year but it was his mother Mrs. Ali who had decreed that her son would finish high school and his father who after twenty three years of marriage was as much in love with the feisty little lady as the day he married her agreed.

NBA scouts eager to grab the next Kobe or Lebron had a hard time understanding how a mother who ran a daycare out of her home and a father who drove a city bus could turn down the guaranteed millions they were offering for their son to play ball on the greatest stage in the world. But turn them down she did and as Bliss cradled the rebound he wondered just how much harder the NBA could possibly be.

His best friend Amir slapped him on the thigh and smiled as they walked to their respective benches for the timeout.

"You doing work kid but you know if you had run with us this would have been a wrap by halftime."

"And if you would just submit to the inevitable I wouldn't have to put in so much work and make you all look so bad."

"Still, two minutes left baby and I ain't heard the fat lady sing yet."

"You right," Bliss said looking up and acknowledging his little sister and her friends in the crowd. At fifteen she was his heart and soul. Bliss knew that if he lost she'd be the one subject to the teasing and harassment of the all the neighborhood kids.

"Beautiful baby. You're doing a beautiful job Bliss. How are you feeling?"

"I'm good coach."

"Good. Okay, DJ we're gonna run a clear out on the left side. You know a little pick and roll just the way we drew it up in practice. Bliss is going to take it down low. We haven't called a play for him tonight so they won't be expecting the play to be called for him.

Bliss I need for you to go hard all the way to the basket. They may foul you which would put us up by three. If they double you and you can't get free kick it back out to DJ or Tony for the three. Take your time. There's plenty of time. If we don't get it get back play good defense and whatever you do don't foul. If they miss and we get the rebound, call timeout. Okay. Hard work on three. One, two, three... HARD WORK!!! Remember it's a two possession game so even if they score remember we'll still get the ball back so don't rush and don't panic."

Coach was a good guy for a White guy and in the time since I'd been there we'd gone 96-1 so I never questioned him. He drew up the game plan and all we had to do was go out there and execute and walk away with the W. It was as simple as that. Only problem was that in those ninety seven wins we had played Jackson only once and of course that was our one and only loss. The only thing on my mind at this point was not to give them neighborhood bragging rights."

"White ball," the ref yelled after blowing his whistle.

"You right about that ref," Amir laughed.

DJ tossed it in to Tony and the five foot eight inch point guard who everyone referred to as Pistol after Pistol Pete Maravich because of his handle and unique ball handling skills slowly and methodically brought it up court with relative ease despite the full court D.

"D up baby," Amir yelled to his teammates. "Watch DJ on the three point line. Don't leave him alone. Stick with him Trey. Don't give him shit," Amir said barking out orders.

The Blue Devils ran their offense like a well-oiled machine. There was no talking, no yelling as DJ took the handoff from Tony and stood at the top of the key where he called out the play before Bliss came to the high post and set a pick which DJ dribbled smoothly around. The pick gave him just enough room between him and his defender that he was momentarily wide open for a three. Both Bliss' man and DJ's man converged on the deadly three point shooter. No sooner did they do this than Bliss cut down the wide open lane. And with split second timing DJ hit him with a picture perfect lob pass. Bliss took the lob with his left hand and slammed it through with Trey draped all over him. The crowd went crazy and the refs whistle could hardly be heard.

"Shooting foul on number thirty two."

Bliss slapped hands with his teammates as he moved to the line.

"What foul?" Trey yelled. "I never touched him. I never touched him. What the hell are you talking about?"

Amir ran over to him and grabbed his teammate.

"C'mon man you can't afford to get T'd up. We can still win this. Just chill. Stay cool man," Amir said grabbing Trey by the shoulders and whispering in his ear.

Bliss stepped to the line.

"That boy got anger management problems," he said smiling at Amir and Trey.

It was no different than the blacktop of the playground where Trey was known to frequently blow his cool. The ref tossed the ball to Bliss when Trey called time out.

"Oh, come on Trey. You might as well get this one over with. You know you can't ice the Iceman. What's a twenty second time out gonna do?" Bliss said on his way to the bench.

"You know I didn't foul you man. That ain't nothin' but these ol' racist refs trying to assure your little White boys the W."

"Why you tellin' me?I didn't call the foul holmes. The ref did. Play the game and respect the man's call."

All but assured the game with a four point lead and thirteen seconds remaining on the clock Coach Marinelli was all but emphatic about the next and what should have been the final play of the game.

"Okay. Bliss makes the free throw we play good strong defense but whatever you do don't foul. No fouls do you understand. Should he miss we don't want to give them the opportunity to hit a three and tie it up so we foul immediately and put them on the line but we get the ball back and just run the clock out. Everyone understand? We're up by three. Bliss makes it no foul. He misses it we foul immediately. Okay. Work hard on three."

Bliss stepped back on the line. Trey was still seething about the foul call and just a muttering away when the ref stepped to him with a firm warning.

"The next comment and I'll hit you with a 'T' young man. Now play ball." Trey dropped his head dejectedly.

"Box out. Box out," Amir yelled to his teammates.

A ninety per cent free throw shooter Bliss took the ball bounced it against the hardwood three times, before touching his ear, for his sister, before bending his knees and lofting the ball softly into the air the same way he'd done thousands of times before only to watch the ball cradle the front of the rim before rolling off. Amir had the rebound and immediately called time out.

"Ball don't lie," Trey shouted referring to the bad call that sent Bliss to the line. "Ball don't lie." He shouted again to no one in particular and was headed to the bench when the whistle blew.

"Technical foul." The ref yelled. "Taunting."

The gym was in chaos as a host of cups and other debris rained down on the court. It was bedlam as both coaches rushed their teams into the locker rooms so their players wouldn't be injured by the hail of objects being thrown or by the angry mob. The police were on the scene within minutes and the place was quickly emptied and order restored.

It wasn't until the next day in school when he was interviewed by the school newspaper when Bliss found out that not only had he broken the all-time rebound record at Immaculate with forty four but he'd also recorded the first triple double in school history with twenty one points, forty four rebounds and thirteen assists.

Now a senior, college scouts were common-place although he paid little or no mind to all of the hullabaloo surrounding his college choice although everyone else seemed to take a special interest. His parents demanded excellence in school and both stayed on him to concentrate on school first and basketball and extracurricular activities afterwards but there was really no need for that. An avid reader since before he could remember; school came easy for him and he maintained an A, B average and was an honor roll student ever since he could remember but like good parents they stayed on him prodding and poking him to do even better.

Still, Bliss was no different than any other seventeen in East New York. A good day for Bliss was spending four or five hours a day down at the park with Amir and Trey. Both young men had already committed to St. Johns not wanting to be too far from home.

It was an unusually warm Saturday morning for November when the boys met at the subway that would take them up to West 4th to a stiffer level of competition. West 4th was where the big boys played.

Some pros, college players and even a legend here or there. And the trio of Bliss, Trey and Amir not only held their own, they held court often times embarrassing the veteran players who had lost a step or two.

"So, you decided on where you're going next year Bliss?"

"Nah man. And if I did you'd be the last person I'd tell Trey," Bliss said pushing his friend off the sidewalk.

"Ah, man I thought we were boys. If you can't tell me who can you tell? I bet you told Amir."

"Bliss ain't told me nothin' yo. And I wouldn't ask. Know what I'm sayin'. That's a personal matter."

"I'm just saying. If all of us went to St. Johns we could put the Big East back on the map and run shit. We could probably go deep in the tournament and by the time we were sophomores we could probably win it all and be a shoe in for the pros. We could go one, two, three in the NBA draft. Of course I'd be the first pick," Trey said crossing over the invisible defender and spinning to hoist a jumper into the air.

"Nigga you trippin'. The only reason you want Bliss to go to St. Johns is so you have someone to carry you and your sorry ass game. And the only thing you gonna be number one is technical fouls. Nigga running around here thinkin' he Rasheed Wallace talkin' 'bout Ball Don't Lie cost us the game."

"I think there was a little more than that that cost you the game, Amir."

"Okay, so you had the game of a lifetime but it was still winnable 'til this Tourette's looking nigga started yellin' Ball Don't Lie, Ball Don't Lie like some fuckin' retard."

All three young men laughed as they descended the subway steps and headed back to Brooklyn. The train was unusually crowded for a Saturday afternoon.

"What's up? Why all the people?" Bliss said staring at both Amir and Trey.

"I think the Nets have an afternoon game."

"That's right I forgot all about that."

"Yeah, my dad just won four tickets to see the Nets play the Clippers the first week in December."

"Chris Paul and Blake Griffin? Damn! I would love to see them boys. CP3 is the nicest point guard in the league if you ask me."

"And who asked you?"

"I'm just sayin'. Rondo may get more assists but Paul has a better handle can go inside and outside. He's a better passer and is clutch."

"Again, who asked you?"

Bliss laughed. He'd known both boys since he was five or six years old and this is how it always had been. They argued over everything from cartoons and who was the better superhero Aqua Man or Spiderman. Bliss had always been the mediator, the ref, the peacemaker. Yet, he knew that the boys loved each other dearly and were incomplete without the other often spending nights at each other's house instead of going home where there was less love and things were almost always off kilter.

Trey had two older brothers that took turns as guests of New York's correction centers for everything from larceny to possession and intent to sell. Bliss couldn't remember how many times five 0 had raided the home and mistakenly picked up Trey thinking it was one of his brothers. It was either Bliss' or Amir's parents that would go down to the local precinct and present proper identification and have him released into their custody. Trey's mother was there but she was one of his brother's prime customers and was so far gone that she seldom knew what was happening in her own house. Well, that was up until Mr. and Mrs. Ali sat down and put everything out there in plain view and on the table and suggested that Trey come live with them. More sober than usual Trey's mother knew that if they took Trey they'd also be taking away her food stamps and one of her sources of revenue. And since she'd already pawned everything else of value she relied heavily on her food stamps which she bartered for more drugs on the first of every month.

Still, Trey managed to stay at Bliss and Amir's far more than he stayed at home. And both households claimed Trey as their own.

"It's a damn shame kids have to be subjected to these selfish no-good trifling parents," Mrs. Ali would remark every time Trey would leave.

"And he's such a good boy and coach says he's doing better than average in all of his classes and his attendance is damn near perfect."

"Yours would be too if you lived under those conditions. Whether you know it or not school is a safe haven for a lot of kids nowadays," Mr. Ali stated matter-of-factly. "Why'd he'd go home anyway?"

"I just think he thought he was wearing out his welcome. Trey's a proud kid you know."

"Why didn't you make him stay?"

"I really don't think he wants to be a burden Samad," Mrs. Ali responded.

"He's no burden. We ain't rich but we have plenty of space and ample food so he wouldn't be a burden just that third child that I always wanted."

Mrs. Ali looked at her husband and smiled incredulously.

"Now this is news to me. I can't ever recall you mentioning anything to me about you wanting a third child."

"It may have slipped my mind but since the cat's out the bag let's go upstairs and practice."

"Mom, pops," Bliss yelled. "Finished my homework and my chores and I'm heading down to the park and probably over to Amir's."

"You askin' or tellin' me?"

"Sorry pops. Can I go down to the park?"

"Son…"

"I know pops. It's a school night so I'll be in early and yeah I'll be safe."

Mr. and Mrs. Ali looked at each other and smiled.

"God is good," Mr. Ali mused to his wife.

"He certainly is," she replied kissing him gently on the lips.

Twenty minutes later Bliss arrived at the park. Stripping down to his sweats he opened his gym bag, took out the worn leather ball and nodded at the crew of ol' men who had made the park their home away from home for as long as he could remember. There was Hawk who was a playground legend and Wild Irish Mike who spent the majority of his day sipping wine of the same name from a brown paper bag and evaluating the local talent and could recite the local history of all the playground talent from Pee Wee Kirkland to Ed Booger Smith who had ever taken to a Brooklyn court.

"Should have been an NBA scout Mike?" Bliss said as he shot jumper after jumper from beyond the arc.

"If I was I would have told Houston not to trade for Jeremy Lin. You know the Knicks ain't got no front office but they made the right decision to let that lil, slow, slant-eyed boy go. I told people that Lin was nothing but a flash in the pan and ain't nobody pay me no mind. They was all caught up in that damn Linsanity but look at him now. Didn't take long or the league to find out that the key to defensing Lin is to make him go left. And since they done figured that out they done all but shut him down."

Bliss smiled at the ol' man's critique but knew that he was right in his deduction.

"You seen Trey or Amir?"

"No can't say that I seen Amir but I did see your boy Trey a little earlier hanging t with some of those no goods."

"No goods?" Bliss said inquisitively.

"Yeah, you know those poison pushers that hanging over there sellin' that shit."

"Trey?"

"Yeah, you look as surprised as I was but I'd know Trey anywhere. He's the boy with the And1 handle and can rein threes on ya like April rain. Boy is as talented a point guard as any one I've seen come out of Brooklyn and that includes Booger and Marbury."

Bliss didn't comment. It was obvious it was all a misperception but to comment about his boy out here in these streets would only be puttin' his name out there on front seat and give those with little or nothing to do fodder for rumors and idle chatter and Bliss as curious as anybody to know the real story wasn't going to do that.

It was unusual that neither Amir nor Trey were here this morning but Bliss went through his usual routine taking five hundred shots from behind the arc and a thousand free throws. He was almost automatic from the stripe but if he missed one he knew there was always room for improvement.

An hour later and still no sign of his boys Bliss packed his bag, waved goodbye to the old men and headed for Amir's.

"How's my baby?" Amir's mother said smiling broadly at Bliss.

"I'm good Mrs. Nelson and you?"

"Everyday I get out of bed I know I'm blessed."

"I know that's right. You sound just like moms."

"Always thought she was a wise woman. I guess you're looking for your boy."

"Yes mam."

"Well, your guess is as good as mine. Got up early this morning and left. I thought he was with you."

"Oh, okay Ms. Nelson you have a good one."

"You do the same and I'll tell him you were looking for him when I see him."

"Thanks m'am."

Bliss found it unusual that not only had he been unable to find either one of his boys and kept to the realization that it could be one thing and one thing only. Girls.

Bliss smiled at the thought. It must have been a pretty good offer from some pretty ass skeezers to keep them from even texting.

Bliss came out of the shower to the shrill voice of his little sister.

"Dag Bliss are you def or what? Tell me you didn't hear your phone ringing? "

Bliss wrapped the beach towel around him and tucked it in then picked up his phone and hit missed calls before heading to his room."

Glancing again at the phone he dressed quickly before returning the call.

"What up Amir? I was at the park."

"Trey got hemmed up. I been wit' him for a couple of hours but I don't know what the fuck is going on wit' this nigga. He actin' all weird and shit and talkin' crazier than usual. I know the nigga better than most anybody and I swear I can't make no sense outta none of it."

"What's wrong with him?"

"I'm telling you the niggas buggin'. It's like he high or been drankin' or somethin'. He ramblin' on 'bout how it ain't worth it and he might as well get paid like everybody else and shit like that."

"Where you at?"

"Over Nikisha's. You know where she stay at?"

"Yeah. Give me fifteen and I'll be there. I'm leaving now."

Couldn't have taken Bliss more than ten minutes to arrive at the petite young girl's house. Hugging her quickly Bliss stepped in the door of the palatial brownstone and followed the girl down the long hallway and to the kitchen. Like all of them, Bliss had grown up with Nikisha and if there were a fourth partner in the crew she would have been it. And where other girls came and went. Nikisha remained a constant and it was only now that she was a junior that she'd put some distance between herself and the other three. As cute as she was she had a hard time finding a date until one boy that she'd taken a particular interest in told her how'd he been threatened by Bliss, Amir, and Trey. Of course, they'd all denied it but it was the same with any boy that took an interest in her. So, she'd cut the chains and put some distance in between herself and her self-appointed bodyguards. They still called her every day and if they didn't see her in and around school they each made their way past her house to check on her. And if they had girl problems she was the first one they sought out. Her mother used to comment that she'd only birthed one child and didn't know how she ended up with four but knew that with them acting as overprotective older brothers she never had to worry about her daughter.

Bliss entered the kitchen and greeted Trey and Amir.

"What's up Trey?" he said staring at Trey after chest bumping Amir who stood just a hair shorter than Bliss.

"Ain't nothin'," Trey replied not baring to look in Bliss' direction.

"Something's up. You weren't at the park this morning. I know you think you're Chris Paul and got a full ride to St. John's but you ain't made it yet nigga so how you just gonna blow off practice. Then when I go there looking for you Mike's gonna tell me that he saw you hanging with the dope boys. What's up fool? I told you that you are not your brother's keeper. The only family you got is right here in this room.

Whatever shit your brother's get into is on them. If they wanna throw their lives away selling that poison then you let them go right ahead but don't you go anywhere near that shit. Them niggas is stupid and will shoot your ass and not think shit about it. Let me catch your ass around them again or even hear about you being around them and I will beat your ass 'til your mama won't recognize you man."

"I already told him," Amir said joining in.

"Shut the fuck up Amir!"

It was seldom that Bliss got angry but it was obvious that he was angry now and Amir stepped back.

"Like I said, I don't know what the fuck you were doing with them boys but that shit is a lose lose situation and everyone here in this room is a winner and we been that way since we were little and I'll be damn if I stand by and watch your ass get caught up in some dumb shit. Damn man."

Trey started to say something but Bliss cut him off.

"Don't say shit to me man. I had some good news for you this morning and find out you talkin' some ol' crazy shit."

For the first time Trey looked up.

"I know you don't think I'm gonna tell you after this bullshit you pulled today," Bliss said staring him in the eye.

"Man, you just don't understand."

"What don't we understand?" Amir asked.

"Man, all three of you guys come from good homes, good families and shit. Man, it ain't like that for me. Every time I go to sleep I gotta put everything I value in my pillowcase or hide it outside somewhere or else one of those motherfuckers done stole my shit and pawned it. I don't know if it's Malik, Jaheim or mom dukes."

"Watch your language Trey mommy's in the front room," Nikisha arned.

"Sorry baby but on the real, ain't none of them niggas worth shit." Trey said lowering his voice. "This morning when I get up my herring bone chain Felicia got me was gone. I sleep with it every night. I don't never take it off. I been goin' with Felicia going on four years and she give me that chain when I first asked her out. Know what I'm sayin'? It's got sentimental value. You know my boo means the world to me. I ain't out here in these streets tryna poke every lil piece of strange my like the rest of y'all."

"That's cause Felicia's the only fool that would have your dumb ass," Amir said laughing at his own joke.

Trey continued as if he hadn't heard his Amir's remark.

"I treasured that chain and don'tcha know those sheisty ass niggas stole my my shit from around my neck. And not only did they steal my chain and my money, they stole my new Jordans coach gave us for tonight's game."

"Damn that is some cold shit," Amir managed not smiling his time."

"That's alright though. I betcha I fixed all that shit. I don't even know who did it. I don't know if it was Malik and Jaheim, mom dukes or one of those shifty ass crack heads they be serving but I know it was because of that shit that I got robbed. But I'll tell you what. And this is real talk. I evened the score up this time cause I'm tired of the shit. I'm tired.

Malik and Jaheim went in on a package of some product and you know they always stashin' the shit in front of me, trying to hide it from moms but you know they don't give a fuck about me 'cause they know I ain't in to that shit so I know where they keep it. They think they can keep boostin' my shit and little brother ain't gonna do or say shit but I'm tired of it. I mean what kind of shit is that? Remember when we used to wear them uniforms at St. Ann's and I had to leave mine at your house just so they wouldn't sell mines. I mean I been goin' through this bullshit all my life."

"So, tell Bliss what your gonna do to rectify this shit, Trey."

"I'm going to get my own place. I don't care if it's just a room where I can rest my head where I ain't gotta worry about somebody stealin' my shit or fiends always being there trying to get high. Even the roaches be hiding there crumbs thinking somebody gonna steal their crumbs and try to smoke it. So, I'm getting'my own spot."

Bliss and Amir's eyes met and both dropped their heads trying to suppress smiles. Any other day they would have busted out laughing but they knew their boy was broke, busted, disgusted and at the end of his rope.

"Nigga got do what a nigga gotta do. It is what it is."

"And how you gonna manage to pay the rent Trey?" Nikisha asked.

"Thought about that too. That's why I stole the package. I'm just gonna keep flippin' the shit until I can get the fuck outta there."

"Man you stupid," Bliss replied but now understanding a little better his friend's grief. "You got pro scouts; I'm talking NBA scouts coming to see you tonight just to see you and trying to get you to go hardship and you talking about flipping some fucking product. The only place that shit's gonna take you is to jail or to your grave. Man you talkin' 'bout tossin' away a four year scholarship to St. John's for a couple of bucks and a room. How you sound? That's crazy as fuck. All it's going to lead to is a bid upstate. Damn man! I thought you were smarter than that."

"Easy for you to say. You live at home with mom and dad and ain't gotta worry about shit. I gotta watch my back out in these crazy ass streets and gotta watch my back in my own goddamn house. That's what's crazy. I can't take it anymore man. I'm tellin' you I gotta get outta there before I go ham on those niggas and kill everybody in the house."

"My nigga talkin' about goin' postal," Amir said busting out in raucous laughter that made everyone including Trey smile.

Bliss interrupted, the concern showing in his face.

"Man you better think about it some more when you're in a better frame of mind. I can understand you going shell this morning. I would have probably acted the same way if I woke up and my shit was missing but I'm telling you the best way to pay those motherfuckers back is to do the right thing and make good. You feel me? If you just go ahead and realize your potential Blackman, shit like a gold chain and a fresh pair of Jordans won't seem like shit. You feel me? And them same motherfuckers wilin' out will be still walking these same ol' grimy streets selling that poison and always trying to stay one step in front of the po po. They'll be so busy looking over their shoulders that they ain't neve gonna be able to move forward. But you can't get down and dirty with 'em Trey. That ain't you. You ain't grimy. Know what I'm saying'"

"I hear you but I gotta do this for me. If I'm ever gonna get any peace I gotta let 'em know I'm not soft just because I'm humble. These niggas take kindness for weakness and those days are over. I love you. You're the only real family I got but this is something I gotta do for me."

"So you gonna throw everything away you've worked for?" Bliss asked making one desperate plea."

"You don't stand for something you'll fall for anything."

"And you think getting' even with these motherfuckers is worth fighting for?" Amir asked.

"The way I feel right now I have to say 'hell yeah'."

Bliss dropped his head.

"Mom and pops were talking last night about your situation and it just so happens that my father said that he'd be glad to have you come and live with us. That was the good news I had to tell you this morning. The offer still stands Trey. If you'd rather not at least have the decency to tell my parents that you appreciate the offer but you have other plans."

"I'll do that but right now I've got some business to take care of. I'll holler at you later my brothas," he said before getting up kissing Nikisha on the cheek and heading towards the door.

The three stood there staring at each other. It was Nikisha who finally broke the silence.

"Why you guys looking so down. You know Trey. He's just blowing off a little hot air. He ain't doin' nothin'. He wants St. Johns so bad he can taste it. He ain't gonna do nothin' to jeopardize that."

"I don't know 'Kisha. The boys over my house at least twice a week and spends two or three nights at Bliss' just so he doesn't have to go home and deal with the madness."

"Real talk, Kisha. I listen to the boy every day and I'm telling you if he didn't have me and Amir he would've been over the cliff a long time ago."

"So you think he's going to go out there and start slingin' and wind up just like his brothers?"

"There's a good possibility the way he's thinking now. He's over the top."

"So why are you just standing there? Get your asses out there and fuck his ass up and get his mind right."

Both young men looked at the petite young lady in front of them and quickly came to the realization that she was right. If there were two people in God's creation that might have a chance it was them.

"C'mon son. Let's go get this fool before he does something crazy," Amir said patting Bliss on the shoulder and heading for the front door.

"What we gonna do when we find him?"

"Don't know. I guess we'll keep taking 'til the nigga gets the message."

"He ain't getting' the message Bliss. He's way past that 'do the right thing and it' pay off in the end shit'."

"You right. If you gotta better plan I'm all ears."

"Nah man. Don't put that shit on me. You the Green Hornet. I'm Kato. I'm just the sidekick baby."

Bliss laughed.

"Where you think he at?"

"Well, you know he can't go home and the school gym ain't open so ain't but two places left and that's over Felicia's house or at the park. And I'm hoping he went to Felicia's."

"Yeah. Me too. My girl ain't goin' for no dumb shit and if she get wind of it you know he gots to give all that crazy shit up."

"That's what I'm hoping."

Two blocks later they arrived at Felicia's house only to find that she had neither seen or heard from him and was worried since he always checked in and let her know his plans.

"This is not like Trey. Do you know he calls me every morning to wake me up and see how I'm doing and well just to tell me he loves me. Trey ain't missed one day in two years."

"Told you the nigga was pussy whipped," Amir laughed. Bliss and Felicia both ignored the comment.

"Is everything okay Bliss?"

"Yeah, everything's cool," Bliss lied.

"Well, when you see him tell him to call me and tell him I'm pissed to the highest passivity."

"I'll relay the message."

"If he don't call you by this afternoon I'll pick up where he left off," Amir laughed.

"Go to hell Amir," Felicia responded smiling as Bliss grabbed Amir's arm and dragged him down the walkway.

"Why didn't you tell her what was up?"

"That's not my place to. Besides what can she do? If she hasn't seen him and he ain't contacted her then she can't do nothing but sit home and worry about his ass. When we find him we'll tell him that she's looking for him and just put that much more pressure on him. You know she ain't going for that shit."

Down at the park there was a full court game that caught Bliss' interest.

"Don't stand there looking like you waitin' for the short bus nigga. Call next so I can whoop your lil sorry ass too," the six eight teen with a game similar to Bliss' yelled out. Bliss smiled at the boy.

"If I didn't have a game tonight I'd make you eat those words," Bliss shouted back.

"Come on baby you can't just let 'em come down to our park and talk shit."

"Why? I ain't got nothing to prove. Them boys ain't shit."

"You're crazy as hell! Ty Sho is averaging twenty-nine and ten and they're undefeated."

"That's 'cause they ain't playin' nobody. What did he have when he played us last year in the playoffs?"

"I ain't sayin' you didn't put the nigga on lockdown but that was last year. This is a whole new year and from what I understand he was up at West 4th everyday this summer and ran in the Rucker and held his own."

"Boy still gets no respect from me. C'mon let's go find Trey."

"No need. He's right there bringing the ball up."

Bliss breathed a deep sigh of relief before heading to the bleachers.

"Foul my ass motherfucker," Trey yelled getting up in some six six players face. This ain't the Catholic school league nigga. You playin' with the pros now son."

"Respect my call nigga. I said you fouled me."

"Take the fuckin' ball out you little pussy," Trey yelled at the boy while flipping the rock to the boy's teammate who immediately passed the ball to the young man yelling foul. Bringing the ball up court against Trey who was all over him now the young man flustered by the relentless pressure dribbled the ball off his ball.

"Good D Trey," Amir yelled catching Trey's attention. Flashing a wide grin Trey turned to Amir and yelled.

"Ball don't lie. Motherfuckin' ball don't lie," he said as he dribbled the length of the court before crossing his defender over twice and launching a three pointer from the top of the key that nestled softly in the net for the game winner.

"Told you. Ball don't lie," he said before grabbing a towel and walking to the sidelines.

"You fellas looking for me?" Trey said smiling and chest bumping both Bliss and Amir.

"Glad to see you're feeling better," Bliss said.

"Never better. Just had to get me a quick run. But I have been thinking. Them college boys ain't ready for me. I'm thinking I may just go hardship so I can get some decent competition. But on the real outside of Chris Paul and Rondo I ain't seeing the competition or the skill level that I possess even in the pros," he said turning the water bottle up and taking a long swig.

"Ty Who?" Bliss commented. "If Trey destroyed these motherfuckers singlehandedly what would happen if the three of us were playing these dudes?"

"I guess you right."

"I'm telling you. You've got to stop believin' the hype."

"I feel you," Amir replied before turning to Trey. "You know you're not supposed to be out here scrimmaging the day of a game.

"First of all, I can run all day and still score thirty and dish out ten or more dimes and you know that. Second of all, I'm not playing tonight."

"You're not what?"

"Can' play barefooted nigga. Didn't I tell you they stole my shoes?"

"You playin' now. What's wrong with the shoes you have on?"

"Man you know how coach is. Everybody's gotta have the same thing on."

"So just run down to Foot Locker and get another pair."

"Nigga if I didn't walk to school with you every day I'd swear you took the short bus. Didn't I tell you the niggas stole my money? And even if they hadn't I still didn't have a hundred and twenty dollars"

"Damn! Them niggas do go hard."

"Who you tellin'?"

"How much you got Bliss?"

"I'm broke. I might have thirty five, forty dollars and you?"

"'Bout the same."

"So, we still forty dollars short plus some tax."

"Let me see if I can get the rest from my pops. He thinkin' Trey's his long lost son anyway. It's fucked up," Bliss laughed. "If I ask him for five dollars I gotta hear how he had to walk five miles and dig potatoes for a nickel a bushel but if Trey needs something ain't no long lectures about the value of a dollar or nothing. Just asks how much and gives his nigga his ATM card and tells him to run down to the store and get what he needs. Am I lying Trey?"

Trey dropped his head and smiled.

"No you ain't lying."

"Makes me wonder if I'm the stepchild or if pops wasn't kickin' it on the side and if Trey isn't really his bastard," Bliss said never breaking a smile.

Both Amir and Trey smiled.

"You smilin' 'cause you know it's true. He does the same thing for you Amir. And for the life of me I can't figure the shit out."

Getting close to Amir's house Amir interrupted.

"I gotta run a couple of errands for my moms. Trey I don't want you going back to the house. You can come in here and shower, change clothes and call Felicia. She's worried about you."

"You seen Felicia?"

"Yeah, me and Bliss was looking for you so we stopped by the crib. Baby girl was looking good too. Started to hit that shit but Bliss was in a rush," he said smiling as Trey threw a stiff jab that Amir ducked before tying Trey up.

"Meet me in an hour at my house," Bliss said before grabbing each man and hugging them as if it were the last time. "And check and see if you can get a few dollars from your mom's Amir."

"I'm already on it."

An hour and a half later the boys exited the Foot Locker.

"Who you playing tonight?" Bliss asked nonchalantly as he did a three sixty trying to get a bird's eye view of the young lady passing.

"And that ain't even close to what we'll be seeing next fall. I'm telling you downtown Brooklyn ain't got nothing on them lovelies out there in Queens.

Know what I'm saying," Trey said swinging his new shoes around and holding out his hand to Amir for some dap.

Amir ignored his friend.

"What the fuck you talking about nigga. You married. Ain't Felicia going to St. Johns? I don't know who's following who?"

"Fuck you Amir. Once I get on campus it's a wrap. Queens is the campus and I'll be all over that bitch. Felicia can't keep tabs on me."

"Yeah, okay," Bliss joined in.

"Nigga you best see all you can see. You gonna probably end up in Osh Kosh By Gosh some fuckin' where looking at White girls with no ass and wishing you had gone to St. Johns," Trey laughed as the three headed down the subway stairs.

"Yeah, okay Trey. But next fall when I see Felicia and your ass walkin' across campus like an old married couple I'm a remind you of all the shit you ran today."

"You must have some pretty good eyesight to see me from the Midwest my brother."

"Where did you get that Midwest shit from?" Bliss asked.

"Well it's either Midwest or down South."

"Says who? You better stop reading all those bullshit papers. The medias speculatin' just like you."

"Don't forget I know you Bliss. And I know you've always been a Michigan and UNC fan so I figure it's got to be one or the other."

"You figure?"

"Got to. Here we are fam and you won't even tell your boys where you're going to college next year."

"That's not true. Amir knows where I'm going. You're the only one that doesn't."

Trey looked at Amir, who stood there smiling and then at Bliss in disbelief.

"Huh uh! I just know you didn't tell this rat toothed grimy, non-shooting motherfucker and didn't tell me."

"Well, if I had it would have been putting it on ESPN and I wanted to keep my options open as long as possible so if a better offer came along I could entertain it. You never know."

"Fuck you Trey. Bliss did the right thing or he would have ended up on TMZ and the world would know."

"And I thought we was cool," Trey said dropping his head dejectedly.

"We are cool Trey. I just didn't want anyone to know. Besides I'll be eighteen next month and if the pro scouts come through and offer me a three year ten million dollar contract pops and mom dukes can protest all they want I'm taking the deal so I don't want to commit too early and miss out on a golden opportunity to get paid. You know what I'm saying so I really didn't want anybody to know. And if I commit to a college and change my mind then they'll be like he's a kid and he's fickled. My credibility and my word wouldn't be shit. So, I had to bide my time but if I do go to college and get the chance to run with you two then St. Johns is my choice."

Trey elated at the news jumped and hugged Bliss.

"Damn! Man we gonna run shit. Fuck UNC and Kentucky. We gonna be the next NCAA champs. You feel me? Plus we got that top rated kid from North Carolina and Ty Sho. And with me running the point ain't gonna be nobody out there close," Trey laughed.

"See Bliss. I told you that nigga was crazy. This morning he wanna be Scarface. This afternoon he think he Magic Johnson. Ain't no tellin' who he gonna be by the time night rolls around. Nigga may think he Obama," Amir added pushing Trey off the curb. "Don't come near me. I don't wanna catch whatever it is you have," Amir laughed pushing his best friend away.

"Who you play tonight?" Bliss asked.

"I don't know," Amir asnswered.

"You don't know who you play?" Bliss asked again almost in disbelief.

"Doesn't matter who we play," Trey replied coming to Amir's defense. "It's not important. What's important is that we're at the top of our game, that we're prepared and that we're fundamentally sound and with our talent level we should come out with the W. You feel me?"

Amir laughed.

"On the real though the competition is none. The only one we're competing with is ourselves. The challenge is to reach our full potential as players and as a team."

"Boy is serious. You ever want Trey to be serious all you have to do is talk b'ball."

"That's cause it's my passion and the key to getting past all the bullshit. So I'm a student of every aspect of the game."

"I hear that," Bliss said smiling.

"See what you niggas don't understand is that you've been blessed with the height that gives you an advantage all the way up until you get to the pro level whereas at six two I'm sure for a point guard in the NBA nowadays so I have to concentrate on m handle, my shot and my D. But while most niggas is sleeping I'm doing all the little things and concentrating on the intangibles that will separate me from the rest of the pack."

"I feel you," Bliss said nodding his head in agreement.

Amir was still smiling.

"Damn if you don't sound like coach. I wouldn't be surprised if Trey ends up coaching somewhere when his playing days are over. Brotha loves some ball."

"I do. It's the only place I feel comfortable."

"There and between Felicia's big, fat thighs." Amir said laughing. "Listen I'm going home and grab a quick nap before the game. You coming Trey?"

"What the hell makes you think I want to go and watch your old ass sleep. You have got to be the oldest young man I have ever seen in my life. This motherfucker makes Rip Van Winkle look like he got ADHD. I swear I ain't never seen nobody sleep as much as Amir. Sometimes I be thinking the nigga dead. Went to see the Brooklyn Nets last week when Jay Z gave the free concert and him and Beyonce came on to do that song they do together."

"Bonnie and Clyde."

"Yeah and I turn around and this niggas snorin'. Now you tell me how a nigga gonna sleep through fine ass Beyonce? Please tell me that? Nigga need some of that Five Hour Energy or something"

"You stupid Trey," Amir said grinning. "Listen. I'll be by about seven to swoop you up."

"Alright my brotha," Bliss said turning to go.

The two walked in silence for a block or so before Bliss turned to Trey.

"What you gonna do about that shit you took from home. I know you ain't still thinkin' about flippin' it?"

"C'mon Bliss. You know me better than that. Why would I sell that poison to anyone? I see what it's done to my own mother. I wouldn't sell that shit to my worst enemy."

"So what you gonna do with it?"

"Ain't really thought about it. I just want them to suffer like I been sufferin'. At first I thought about flushing it but I know it ain't theirs and I really ain't tryna see nobody get fucked up or killed. I just wanna see 'em sweat. Might make 'em think about fuckin' with me."

"So what did you do with it?"

"Stashed it."

"You know they gonna be lookin' for you."

"No doubt but what they gonna do? I ain't worried about Malik or Jaheim,"

"You better be worried about the man they got it from."

"Nah son. They ain't gonna say nothin' cause the man will be on them. They're the ones responsible for the package."

"I hear you. I just hope you know what you're doing. You're playing a dangerous game Trey. Why don't you just go home and give them the package."

"Nah son. I got a game to play tonight and I don't want no drama before the game. Besides they can sweat for a couple more hours and I'll give it to them after the game."

"Alright Trey."

"Let me get a quick game of Madden before I lay it down."

"Who you got?"

"Jets baby with Tebow starting."

Two hours later, Bliss sat in the bleachers behind the home team as Trey and Amir took the floor. Due to injuries Amir was starting at center instead of his usual power forward position but at six six and a half he still dwarfed his defender and could care less as long as he got his minutes. Trey at six two was the very vocal starting point guard and floor leader. They were the stars and the rest of the supporting cast were made up of local ballers whose skill level was better than most.

No sooner had they taken the court than Trey's words rang out in his ears. The Blue Devils ran their sets almost as though they were the only team on the floor with Trey pushing it up the court with controlled abandon each time he touched the ball while Amir's rebounding initiated fast break after fast break. At the end of the first the scoreboard read 44-18.

It was a clinic and yet Coach Smith still found reason to bitch. The second quarter proved no different and several times Bliss found himself on his feet screaming and yelling. On one break Amir rebounded gave the outlet pass to Trey who headed up court with blinding speed and threw a no look alley oop to the trailer who was none other than Amir for the flush. For Bliss there was nothing better. It was like And1 and Rucker combined. Taking his cell out, he flipped on the camcorder on his cell whenever Trey touched the ball. And even though he had no way of predicting what would happen next every other play could have made ESPN's highlight reel. There was the one play where Trey's defender doing his best not to be embarrassed by the talented point guard thought he was tightening up his D and Trey crossed him over so quickly that he left his defender on his ass and went down the lane for an uncontested dunk. The crowd went wild and Bliss wondered if Trey's predictions about winning the NCAA Championship weren't too far off base. Looking to the right now Bliss recognized several NBA scouts and for the first time in his high school career he found himself unnerved by their mere presence. 'Leeches' he thought to himself and realized his mother's words about them being intent on exploiting the poor and desperate with the lure of big money and promises. Colleges did the same thing without the money but she was right. They gave you something no one could ever take from you. And that precious commodity was an education.

The revelation was as clear as a church bell on a Sunday morning and he now knew that there was little question as to where he would be next fall. And the thought of finally playing with his two best friends excited him greatly. It would be just like playing in the park except now they would be on the big screen receiving the recognition they'd worked their whole lives for. He was happy about his decision and felt like a weight had been lifted. The fourth quarter was winding down and looking over at the scorer's table he saw that Amir had his usual solid game with twenty eight points, fourteen rebounds and six blocks. And it occurred to him that if anyone could motivate Amir he could dominate games much in the same way he and Trey could but the fact remained that Amir, probably the most talented of the three had always been laid back and reserved. And no matter what anyone did to prod him to be more aggressive it just wasn't in his makeup. And yet he remained a solid pro prospect.

Yet, where Amir's stat line was good, Trey's was unbelievable. And for the seventh time in eight games he had recorded a triple double with thirty six points, nineteen assists and eleven steals. More importantly he was six of seven from beyond the arc. The pro scouts were drooling and although several approached Amir the vast majority were intent on inking Trey to a contract write then and there.

Forty five minutes later Amir and Trey emerged from the locker room to find Bliss shooting threes.

"Beautiful game baby," Bliss said to both. "That shit was devastating. Made everything clear to me if ya know what I'm saying." Then turning to Trey Bliss said. "I really believe we can transform St. Johns back into a powerhouse so I'm gonna put all my thoughts of the pros on the back burner and run with you fellas for the next couple of years."

"That's what I'm talking about baby," Trey said hugging Bliss. "We just getting warmed up for better days baby."

Amir smiled but said nothing.

"As for you Big Man. Me and Trey gonna find a way to light a fire under your ass. You could probably have had fifty if you were just a little more aggressive. And that's not to say that you didn't dominate but damn Amir with your talent you should be the man."

"That's what coach keeps tellin' this fool," Trey added.

"Pops is always telling me that the worst thing in life is wasted potential," Bliss commented as the three young men stepped out into the brisk fall air as shots from an automatic weapon rang out.

Mama's Friend

"What's up, yo?" The clean cut young man with the fresh fade approached his best friend a broad smile reaching across his dark brown face.

"Ain't nothin'. Same ol', same ol'. You know. What's up with you Vaughn? I know you saw your boy, A.I. last night?"

"No doubt. You know I don't ever miss Allen Iverson or the Nuggets when they're on. That's my man. Broke the Piston's off something proper-like, didn't he? He's got one helluva crossover dribble doesn't he? I saw him cross Chauncey and Tayshaun over in the first quarter. Made 'em look stupid—damn near ridiculous."

"For sure. They can't do nothin' with him. Just imagine if he had a better supporting cast to take some of the scoring load off of him."

"Whaddaya mean? Hell, he's got Carmelo to help him." The dark-skinned round-faced boy said to his friend, DJ.

The two boys had been best friends for as long as either of them could remember and it wasn't uncommon for one to start a sentence and the other to finish it, but not when it came to basketball where both knew that they were the supreme authority on the subject.

"Carmelo? I know you're not talking about 'Melo helpin' to shoulder the load. *Man please.* 'Melo's always been soft. That's why Denver ain't going nowhere."

"Man, how can you say that? You know the boy's injured. I really think he came back too soon. You know it takes more time to come back from an injury like that."

"Whatever. But I remember when he wasn't injured and he still played soft in the playoffs. That's why Denver never ever had no real chance. Instead of playing hard-nosed basketball, like a true power forward he's up there taking jumpers from the top of the key like he a point or a shooting guard or some shit. That's why I say he's soft. It's like he doesn't wanna mix it up down low with the big boys. Maybe he's scared. I don't know. But your boy Allen will mix it up with the best of 'em. Allen don't fear nobody. He'll mix it up with the best of them."

"For sure. A.I. plays a lot whole helluva lot bigger than five-ten. I'll say that for him. And it ain't like he got this enormous wingspan like Rasheed or

Tayshaun. He just got heart. Hell, he ain't even as tall as you are, Vaughn. How tall are you anyway? You gotta be about six 'cause I'm five-nine. Shit, come to think of it, your ass should be dunkin' big as you are," DJ laughed, "Lose some of that weight and you probably could," DJ said runnin' from his friend.

"Fuck you, DJ!"

"Ah, man you know I was only bullshittin' but on the real if I had your height I'd be slammin' on niggas left and right," he said stealing Vaughn's dribble then spinning left before hoisting the ball high at an imaginary hoop before catching the rebound and passing the ball back to his friend.

At close to six feet and weighing nearly three hundred pounds, Vaughn was the bigger of the two and also the quieter with an easygoing personality that made it seem like he gave less than a care about anything. Well, that was anything except for basketball and his dream of one day playing in the NBA. Neither could pass for a choirboy and both stayed in more trouble than either cared to think about and it was nothing for them to skip school to go across town to play ball. Walking along, Vaughn broke the easy silence with a thought. The thought was a recurring one and one that hardly ever left his mind.

"You know, I don't give LeBron a lot of props but Iverson's different. Did you hear what Rip Hamilton of the Piston's said about him? Said Allen had the heart of a lion. He knew that when A.I. was with Philly they didn't have a chance in hell of beating the Pistons but Allen pushed them to the limit each and every time he got the ball in his hands—even when his teammates didn't show up at all. It was almost like his teammates gave up before the series even started. They was like—'wow we're playing the World Champion Detroit Pistons. We can't beat them'. Almost like they was intimidated by all the hype and hoopla and 'cause the Pistons got all those stars. But Allen didn't care. Even when they were down three games to one, he still played like it was game one and it was anybody's series to win. That's the way I'm gonna be when I get to the NBA."

"When you get to the NBA? Hell, nigga you can't even get outta the house let alone get to the NBA. You know your momma's boyfriend got yo' ass on lockdown. You bout the only nigga I know in Harlem that don't never make parole or get no time off for good behavior. Every time I see you he's got you locked up for something or another. That's why yo' ass wanted to skip today. That's the only way you get to see what the outside world is like.

But on the real though, Vaughn, I don't see how you let this punk ass walk into your crib outta the clear blue and start tellin' you what to do. I couldn't do it but I give the boy his props. He one helluva of a playa. He screwin' both you and your moms at the same time. Two women in the same house. Now that's what I call a true playa for real. I don't even think my man, Q could pull off some shit like that and he 's the biggest hustla in Harlem," DJ said laughing and moving out of his friends' path at the same time.

"Fuck you, DJ," Vaughn said the anger obvious in his voice.

"Ahh, come on man, I was just joking he said apologetically now sorry he'd said anything after looking at his friend's face.

Vaughn smiled an uneasy smile followed by a lull. There was a silence but it was a comfortable silence, the kind that came with friends who'd known each other all their lives and could never be offended or hurt by the other regardless of what the other said or did. Still DJ's words hadn't fallen on deaf ears and Vaughn's only thoughts were of momma's boyfriend who had moved in once again and for who knows how long this time. Each time he moved in he promised momma that this was it. This was the final time and whatever it took, they would make it this time. No matter what happened, they would make it. A month or two later, momma would be in tears all over again and Todd would be long gone. But he wasn't the only one. He was just this month's savior and hero.

Vaughn could remember the men that had passed through and he'd always been receptive, always trying to get along, hopping that this one

would be the one that put a smile on momma's face and keep it there. But no matter what he did to help the situation they never stuck around long.

Todd was different though. He'd really liked Todd in the beginning. But no matter what he did or how hard he tried to get along with the man something would inevitably go wrong. As soon as things seemed to be going along smoothly he'd always managed to do something stupid and get caught red-handed like the time he stole Todd's precious cd's and DVD's and took them to school and sold them. Or the time he'd picked up the change on momma's dresser without asking. Hell, it was bad enough that momma never had any extra money to buy him any new clothes and when she did she refused to spend it on buying him the stuff that everyone else was wearing because it was always too expensive according to her. And she sure as hell wasn't spendin' no hundred dollars on no damn tennis shoes just so he could look like every other lil' thug runnin' the streets. That's what she would tell him.

What was even worse was the fact that he had to stand in that stupid line at school for kids receiving reduced lunches. These were the lunches that were usually for the kids receiving public assistance or welfare and even when he was in this line he never had the forty cents for that. He'd thought about joinin' DJ and a couple of his partners down on the corner sellin' rock but Lord knows he wasn't sure about that but if things got much worse... Anyway, he just didn't know right through here. Hell, everybody was doing it but slingin' dope was always the beginning of the end. He'd seen too many bad things happen around drugs. And he still had a future ahead of him.

So, he didn't think there was anything wrong with taking the dollar or two in change that momma used to leave up there on top of her dresser. And she never said anything about it and she had to know he was taking it even though she never mentioned it but then Todd had come along and all of a sudden it was a big thing. Well, maybe he should have asked. But if he knew momma like he thought he knew momma she wasn't going to say anything but no if he asked her and like he said he hated being with the low-income kids when he knew momma was just too cheap to pay. But Todd said that taking the money without asking was the same as stealing and had made a fuss and then momma had made a fuss although she didn't really make a big fuss. She just kinda of supported Todd because he was the only man that really and truly acted like he loved her.

He'd never really expected anyone to find out though, until one day he picked up Todd's change instead of momma's and being that Todd was broke all the time he counted the few pennies he had. Matter-of-fact, it surprised Vaughn that Todd wasn't rich since he knew everything about being a strong Black man and every other subject that came his way.

At least he pretended to know something about everything just because he used to be a schoolteacher. He'd given up teaching to write. But after receiving rejection after rejection he'd grown tired and frustrated and now he couldn't even get his old position as a teacher back. So, now he was broke and evil most of the time. And it just seemed like any ol' thing would set him off.

Vaughn remembered when Todd had first come into their lives. He was seven or eight when momma first brought him home and he seemed like a pretty cool dude at first but one thing was obvious from the git-go.

Todd didn't like him. Not one bit, not even from the start when he hadn't done anything to make him dislike him. Vaughn didn't know if it was because he was fat or if it was because he was a little loud or because Todd just wanted momma all to himself. All he knew was that Todd never liked him although if he had a sip or two and wasn't screamin' and shoutin' at momma they would get along pretty good. But as the years went on and after he'd gotten caught stealing Todd's shit on a couple of occasions it just seemed like there was nothing he could do to make Todd like him, so he'd just given up and said 'fuck it'.

Besides he had no idea why he did the things he did. Fact of the matter was he never even thought about it. He didn't know why he stole stuff. He sure didn't want to be no hoodlum or go to jail or make momma be upset with him. He didn't understand it himself. He just did it. His older sister, Jasmine had done the same thing. And when momma couldn't take no more and Jasmine was sixteen momma put her out. But that was different. By the time she was sixteen, Jasmine had been arrested something like twenty-six times for larceny and been in and of jail and boot camps and even though momma had put her out she kept doing the same things over and over again. And then there was daddy. Vaughn had never met the man but from all of momma's accounts his daddy had been in jail most of his life. He'd come out fathered him then done something and gone right back in. Daddy had done everything from kidnapping, attempted murder to armed robbery and that was just to name a few. He'd even overheard momma say that, 'maybe it was something in his genes when he'd gotten in trouble the last time. So, maybe that was it. Maybe he and Jasmine got it honestly but he certainly wasn't trying to be no hoodlum or no jailbird like Jasmine and daddy.

Vaughn thought about the night he'd heard momma and Todd arguing. It wasn't hard to hear them since their bedroom was right next to his and something he'd heard made him get up to get a closer listen. Standing outside momma's bedroom door, it was soon apparent what had gotten his attention. They were talking about him. Well, at least Todd was. Recently, he'd become Todd's favorite topic of conversation and as loud as Todd was talking it was obvious that he didn't care one little bit whether he heard it or not.

"If he was my son, I'd beat his ass. And as if it's not enough that you ask me to put my own two kids on the back burner and be a part of your life and make this my home is one thing. But the fact that I can't put anything down or leave something lying around for fear of it growing wings and getting ghost is a whole 'nother thing altogether."

The large, buxom woman sat there unable to answer while Todd went on-and-on ranting and raving. Vaughn, still standing outside the door, wondered why it was that some people seemed so taken by the sound of their own voices.

"I'm not saying my kids are perfect but I sure don't have to be a prisoner in my own house or lock my shit up for fear of it being stolen. You're too damn easy on him, sweetie and he's walking all over you. This shit is ridiculous and you baby him so much and refuse to listen any advice that it's no wonder he does the things he does.

The boy can't write a goddamn sentence and he's in the ninth grade. What's worst is he's scared to go to school 'cause these little punks are runnin' 'round here threatenin' to beat his ass for some shit he got into of his own accord. And when I finally get you to go down to the board to see if you can have him transferred everyone down there knows him as a gang affiliate, whatever the hell that means.

I'm not even sure that I know what that means but whatever it means, it sure as hell ain't good. Then they go on to tell you that the boy's been selling bootleg cd's and DVD's in school which just happen to be mine and you come home in tears, looking like you just lost your best friend.

Shit! The only one that should've been crying is Vaughn. Should have worn his ass out right then and there, right on the spot. Come on baby! Wake up and smell the coffee! You keep trying to play everything off and hoping for the best, but the best only comes from putting forth the effort, baby. Hoping and praying is fine but until you put a foot in his ass you ain't really doing shit on his behalf except avoiding the problem and reinforcing his behavior. You think quiet is good but trust me there's always quiet before the storm.

You might want to seriously consider getting the boy some help. I've worked with a lot of children in the last twenty years—kids that were considered incorrigible, with every kind of problem. I've worked with children that were considered behaviorally challenged, sexual offenders, violent offenders... You name it, if there was a negative label placed on a child, I've worked with them and I'll tell you the God's honest truth I've never worked with anyone like him. Maybe, it's because I'm older now. Maybe, it's because I'm in such close proximity and maybe it's simply because I can't get up and walk out at five o'clock and leave the problems behind me. I don't know. But if there's one thing I do recognize it's the fact that the boy needs help. And you really need to concern yourself with that before the problem gets out of hand. But go ahead. Keep sweeping shit under the rug. It's only a matter of time before you can't hide it anymore. The fact of the matter is the boy has got some pretty deep-seated problems.

And whether you know it or not baby, I'm not meaning to sound harsh but I ain't so much worried about his dumbass as I am about yours. He's not showing you any courtesy or respect. And to tell you the truth I'm not so much interested in what's wrong with him as I am with you. I just have a hard time understandin' why you don't put your foot in his John Brown ass. The nigga needs a goddamn wake up call. Then as if that ain't enough, the White folks down at the school are happy to tell you that this sorry-assed, stupid motherfucka is the one responsible for your house being broken into, *not once, not twice but three times in a month. In a month!*

I'm sure glad I wasn't around at the time all this shit went down. I swear I am. I would've tried to kill somebody. And what's more, I can't believe you had the nerve to call and tell me. Talkin' about you came home and went to put a movie in the DVD player and there was no player and he was home all day but he doesn't know what happened to it. Please. That would have been it right there. But no, you're gonna wait 'til he decides to come clean. I'll be damned. You'll be old and gray by the time that happens. Wait 'til he comes clean. *I'll be damned! But hey, he's not my son. Thank God!!*

You should have been too embarrassed to let anyone know especially since you're allowing him to still live there. Trust me. *Normal* people don't have the problems you have with children. I mean, we all have problems with our children but no one has problems of this magnitude on a regular basis. I mean this shit is not a once in a lifetime thing. Every week it's something. Every single week it's something and you keep telling me that you ain't wit' all the drama. But you allow the drama to come into your house. Your house! Your house which is supposed to be your safe haven from the madness of the outside world. But you've got the madness right here where you rest your head.

Damn! You went through the same thing with your daughter. I mean a bad seed is one thing and everybody knows that kids will be kids but when you start talking about criminal activities from not one but both kids then there's something definitely wrong. I've worked with kids most of my adult life and trust me there comes a time when we as adults, as parents have to step up to the plate and acknowledge that there are some serious problems."

Vaughn knew that everything Todd was saying was true but if she'd let it go then why couldn't he. Always bringing up the same old shit like it happened yesterday. Always talking about things that happened in the past.

The robberies were months ago but Todd just couldn't let it rest. Always walking around talking about what it takes to be a strong Black man and all of that garbage. But he wasn't doin' nothin' but livin' off of momma, eatin' her food and running up the electric bill and pretendin' to be uppity. Hell, in the seven years he'd been dating momma I can only remember him having one job and that only lasted about two weeks before he quit. And he the one always talkin'about bein' a strong Black man.

Hell, what kind of man has a wife and two kids that he don't support and goes to see whenever he gets ready and then when he gets mad over there comes and lays down with momma.

I know he's screwin' momma 'cause I'm right in the next room and I can hear her holler when he hits her sweet spot. That's what they call it when it feels real good to them and they start screamin' and moanin'like momma be doin' all the time. Sometimes I can hear him hollerin' too and momma tells him to hush but a couple of minutes later I hear him sayin' all kinds of stuff that I don't really wanna hear like him tellin' my momma what to do in the bedroom.

One time, when I was like nine or ten, his daughter came over and spent the night with us, me and her was standing by momma's door listening and heard everything. I told momma what I heard 'cause me and momma's a lot alike and we both laughed about the whole thing but when she told him later on he didn't think it was real funny. He never thinks anything I say is real funny. I guess he figures that one day I might learn somethin' I shouldn't from listenin' to them in the bedroom. Either that or he don't feel comfortable sleepin' in the bed with momma in front of me and they ain't married. That goes along with all that 'be a strong Black man' shit. Stuff like that bothers him a lot but me and momma don't really think about stuff like that. At least I don't. But then again, I guess I kind of understand because I really don't like him being in the bedroom with momma all the time like I'm sure he wouldn't want me in the bedroom with his daughter all the time.

Sometimes, I don't think he really likes the way things are with him and momma screwin' all the time with me being around to see it. I think figures that if he leaves and momma brings another man around or starts seeing other men and they go in her bedroom too much then that's not a good image for me to see 'cause I'll think that that's all women are for. At least that's what I overheard him tellin' momma one day when he thought I wasn't listenin'. But when she calls him and says, 'C'mon Todd!' he just drops his head and says—kind of embarrassed like—and then goes to see what she wants. And we both know what she wants. But like I said, I don't think he likes doing that and at the same time trying to show me what a strong Black man is s'pozed to act like. But then I know he loves her 'cause he puts up with a lot of her shit. And I guess he figures that if she don't care then why should he? After all, I ain't his son.

Most of the time though it ain't like we don't get along. Most of the time we just sit around and talk or watch the game together. Like I said we really get along pretty good 'til I do something stupid and he makes a mountain out of a molehill over it. But most of the time though he just talks to me and tell me stuff that he thinks is gonna help me when I get older. And most of the time I listen to him seems 'cause I think he really cares about what he's saying like he's passionate or sometimes, I even think he wants me to grow up and be stronger than he is and that's why he tells me stuff so I wont make the same mistakes he did. And sometimes, he even thinks it's like he just gets real mad and real angry cause I'm not getting what he's saying quick enough or he feels like momma is letting him do all the child rearin' just to 'cause she's too into her own self to do it and just wants to get me outta her hair.

Sometimes, I think that momma thinks that as long as she does her job in the bedroom and brings in the groceries that he can have the job of making me turn out alright but a lot of the times I don't think he wants the job and momma can go too if he gotta be a father to me full-time.

And since all momma does is work and after all the trouble and the problems she had with my sister I don't really think she wants the job either. But she don't mind taking care of my sister's baby cause she still a baby and she's still cute and light-skinned and all but me on the other hand I'm pretty big just like momma and everybody says we favor but she's a woman and I know that down deep she really wishes that she was skinny and pretty like them girls on the videos so men would like her more and she wouldn't have to put up with Todd's ol' evil ass. But she ain't. She's fat just like me and I think that's another reason she don't wanna be around me since I remind her so much of herself and all the things she don't like about herself.

I know that momma loves me but if it's a choice between workin' or havin' to be a parent she'd probably choose workin' nine times outta ten. And mostly that's what she did before she got laid off last week. Basically that's all she ever did. Just worked. So, I had to take care of myself everyday since I was a little kid. But that ain't really nothing new since I been takin' care of myself since I was nine or ten. But when the house got broken into and her and Todd tried to work things out for the thousandth time, it was like all of a sudden I got a new parent or something and he just came struttin' up in here expectin' me to do stuff my own mother don't ask me to do.

Then he tells me he's gonna show me how be a strong Black man and a good student and stuff like that. But maybe I don't wanna be a strong Black man or a good student. I'm not saying that I don't wanna be. I'm just sayin' that he never asked me he just sorta shoves it down my throat like that's what everyone's s'pozed to do. And I'm thinkin' things to myself the whole entire time he's talkin'. Don't strong Black men have jobs? Don't strong Black men feed themselves? Don't strong Black men have cars? Don't strong Black men take their women out every now and then? Do strong Black men live off of women?

I think that's why he hated the word 'pimp' so much. Guess it reminded him of someone he knew.

Anyway, one day I just asked him. I just said, "Todd can I ask you a question?"

And he said, "Yeah. Sure. Go ahead."

He liked it when I asked him questions. Guess it made him feel important and some people just naturally need to feel important so, I said "Todd," even though momma thought I should call him Uncle Todd caused that showed respect. Most of the time I wouldn't call him by name at all if it meant me havin' to call him Uncle Todd.

Anyway, I said, "Todd. With all your college education and all your teachin' experience and all the books you've read and all the time you spend studyin' and on the computer and in the library then how come you can't keep a job?"

I mean I was respectful and everything but I guess I must've hit a nerve 'cause when momma came home he told her what I said and that was all she wrote.

Momma went off on me like I had just killed somebody and I knew right then and there that one of us had to go. That was the final straw. First of all, I hadn't said anything that wasn't true. Second of all, I got tired of this nigga comin' in off the street anytime he got ready to and actin' like he knew every fuckin' thing like he was some goddamn genius or something. And half the time he couldn't even afford to buy himself a pack of cigarettes. Momma had to buy them for him or else he smoked all of hers and as much as she smoked she wasn't havin' that. But the thing that really got me was that she took his side against me—her own son. Right then and there was when I decided it was time for him to go.

Up 'til that point I really didn't care if she locked me out of her bedroom and spent all her time in there letting him screw her brains out like I didn't know what was going on. Most of the time I was watching T.V. or eatin' or hangin' out so I didn't really care what they did as long as they didn't bother me.

And since she seemed pretty happy with the situation I didn't care but lately he was actin' too much like he cared or wanted to be my daddy or something and I didn't need him to be my daddy since I already had one even if I ain't never seen him. But even when I lied and told her that I didn't know who stole the DVD player or who broke into our house she never really said or did anything. But when I said I insulted and disrespected him 'cause I told the truth about him not being able to keep a job, she gonna tell me—her own son—that I needed to get out, 'cause she wasn't going to allow me to disrespect her man. Now picture that.

Even when he wanted to know why I packed up all of his DVD's and put them in the desk drawer next to the back door and left the back door open, momma lied and covered for me sayin' that she must have forgotten to lock it. She didn't even get upset when he asked her what happened to the bike that he gave me for my birthday and I just played it off and told it I left it at a friend's house. Actually, I didn't expect her to act any differently than she did when I got and sold the bike she bought me. I just told her about that one when she asked me she didn't get too upset. She just told me that I needed to take better care of my things and by the next day everything was back to normal and cooler than a fan.

Hell, if Todd hadn't been there she would've never noticed half the shit that was missing since she don't half pay attention to what I'm doin' most of the time. And it ain't because she don't love me. It's just that with her bein' busy with tryin' to work and feed me and my niece and all she just don't have the time to be worryin' about what I was doin'. Not even when he told her that I stole some of his cd's—which I did—she really didn't get too upset. She just covered for me the same as she always did and hoped and prayed that I would stop all the dumb shit. Of course, by now I really didn't care. I was pretty much tired of him tryin' to run things and play daddy and always assignin' me chores and books for me to read. He had even gotten to the point where he thought he had to check my homework behind me. I don't know if he was tryin' to help me or if he was tryin' to open momma's eyes and show her just how bad a parent she was but one thing was for sure neither her nor me wanted that shit rubbed in our face.

Like I said she was doing the best she could considerin'. And what he didn't understand was that as bad as things were momma always wanted to believe that things were okay even if that was the farthest thing from the truth. Here we is livin' smack dab in the middle of Harlem but if you didn't know any better and you talked to momma you would swear we lived smack dab in the middle of Beverly Hills. You see, bad as things were momma really wanted to believe that things were okay. She's what my English teacher; Miss Dunleavy calls an 'optimist'.

At the same time, he's still insisting on me being a strong Black man like his father and his son. And that I really don't need to hear and neither do momma. Ain't doin' nothin' but putting pressure on me and momma. That's all he's doin'. Just puttin' pressure on me and momma.

After all, how many Black men do you see sittin' around readin' and bein' all studious and shit? That's like a White person's dream. It's almost like he wanna be White or somethin'. I'm sorry but when I go outside I don't see nobody standin' around readin' and actin' all pretentious. Well, except the Muslims and everybody know they crazy as hell. Hell, me and momma was perfectly happy before he got here just sittin' around watchin' television and snackin' and just basically, chillin' and relaxin'.

That's why after thinkin' about the situation for awhile I decided that he definitely needed to be on his way 'cause he was never gonna be content to just stay in momma's room and fuck her. No, DJ was right. He wasn't happy just screwin' her. He wanted to screw me too and up 'til then I was pretty happy just doin' what I was doin' which was basically nothing.

Well, he must have really loved momma 'cause I put that fool through pure hell and he did his best to hang in there even though I know it was eatin' away at him. But you know for me it wasn't really hard. You see, I'm basically lazy and I just went back to doing things the way I had before he got here with all his highfalutin' and uppity ways. Anyway, like I said I went back to doin' things the way I'd always been doin' them and if he asked me to do somethin' I would but I would do it of my own accord and in my own sweet time. Then I'd do it half-assed just the way I did things before he got here. Well, I could see that this was driving him crazy 'cause he really and truly thought he was starting to make some progress with me. But in my heart I knew it was just a matter of time because everybody says I'm a pretty hard case. And I was right. After awhile, he stopped telling me what to do or what it took for me to become a strong Black man, and a role model and a pillar of society and all that other shit I wasn't the least bit interested in becoming.

At one point, he even turned to me and said that he was here to stay and if one of us was leaving it wouldn't be him. That's when I knew I had him. That's about the time he started drinkin' heavy again and ignorin' me altogether.

Momma could see what was happenin' and so she started tryin' to pick up the pieces where Todd left off 'cause she thought I was comin' around too and changin' for the better since he'd been there. In her eyes, and if nothin' else, at least the house stayed clean when Todd was around. And I gotta admit that he did teach me how to cook a couple of new dishes. But when momma started sittin' down with me every night to help me with my homework and he stayed in the bedroom not hardly showing his face whenever I was around I started counting the days. And I knew right then and there that I wouldn't have to count too much longer.

Funny thing though, I really wanted him to go so everything could get back to normal with me and momma but I really started to miss all the talks me and Todd used to have when it came to basketball. Now, I gotta admit that as much as he got on my last nerve he did know a whole helluva lot when it came to basketball. And I mean a whole helluva lot. And that was the thing—the one thing—that I did miss. Still, I pretty much figured on was the fact that he'd already raised his own son and I knew he really wasn't wanting to start over with a hard case like me except for the fact that he loved momma and couldn't see me doin' nothin' to hurt her. And I also knew that he was missin' his own kids somethin' awful. And to him it just didn't make any sense workin' with me and I didn't want to learn when there were other kids out there, includin' his that wanted to learn. At least that's what I overheard him tellin' momma. Besides that he was always complainin' about me not doin' nothin' and not wantin' nothin' out of life. He said that was hurtin' momma too even though she didn't show it.

And all the while this stuff is taking place, momma was tryin' to explain to him that I didn't get like this overnight and I wasn't goin' to change or get to wherever the hell he thought he was taking me overnight either. Now, either he didn't believe that or maybe he just didn't understand. I don't know. But he just kept pushin' me to do better.

Todd don't seriously believe I'm ever gonna do anything earth-shattering to make momma proud of me. And to tell you he truth, I don't think momma believes I'm gonna do much either. I think she gave up on me a long time ago but as long as I don't have any kids out-of-wedlock, for her to raise like my sister did and I don't follow in my daddy's footsteps and go to jail then I guess in her eyes if I don't do none of those things, and I get a job, and graduate from high school then I'm pretty much a success. Especially if I can get a job and take care of myself and not be in and out of work and always relying on public assistance like she has to. And so far,

I've been pretty good, being that I've only been arrested once and here I am almost sixteen.

That's why I say ain't nobody thinkin' about college and careers and all that 'cept for little White kids and uppity niggas like Todd and his boy. He thinks that just 'cause everybody in his family graduated from college and he got his son down at Chapel hill on a academic scholarship and he got family in another country that that makes him Big Willie and everybody's s'pozed to follow in their footsteps and go to college. But I'll tell you what, all that stuff don't mean a hill of beans up here in Harlem. The only 'Big Willie's' up here are the ballas and shot callas. Either you make a name for yourself playin' ball or you're hustlin' and got some clout and you're the ones callin the shots. Those is the onliest ones getting' any respect 'round here. Those are the ones drivin' 'round in Escalades and Benz's with spinners and makin' the real dough. They ain't just talkin' and bullshittin'.

Besides, my momma ain't never finished college and she ain't doin' too bad. We live in a nice apartment and got a big screen television and everything. And we always had a car. And some nice one's too. And with all f Todd's education he don't even own a car. I mean he did but he don't now. But we always had a car. So why he thinks college is so important, I just don't know. That's not to say that I ruled it out altogether. I still might go but that's only if I don't go to the NBA. But like I said before, college and the future just ain't nothin' I'm feelin' right now. And if they ain't got no college right here in Harlem I don't know if I'll ever go 'cause really I ain't never tryin' to leave Harlem. You can call it the ghetto if you want but I love it. I love it here.

Oh, I been other places like in the summers when I was a kid and my grandma was livin'. Momma used to always send me down to North Carolina to spend the summer vacation with her and my cousins so I wouldn' be out there in the streets 'cause she say the streets ain't nothin' but trouble. And it was okay. I mean I had fun but it wasn't nothin' like Harlem so I just don't know. I ain't really been nowhere else but if the rest of the world's like North Carolina then I'd rather stay right on up here in Harlem. Besides everybody knows me and ain't too many people really gonna mess with you if they know you're a stand up guy. I can go right outside my building right now and somebody'll pass me a blunt or I could even go to work 'cause the older cats got a lot of respect for me and the way I carry myself but they recognize I got a future so they really don't push me to do nothin' but stay in school and keep playin' ball.

Anyway, if I do go to college, I think that I'll probably go to Duke since they got a pretty good basketball program and I like their uniforms. Still, there ain't really no rush to decide right now and I'll be damned if I'm going to let somebody tell me what I'm going to do when I've been doing pretty good on my own up 'til now. But Todd he don't see none of that. He even went so far as to buy me a Duke cap and got happy when I mentioned Duke then tol' me what I needed to get in and—well—I might not go if I gotta have four years of straight A's 'cause I already messed up my freshman year but I still like their uniforms 'cause blue's my favorite color. He even got me in a better high school where there ain't no crews or gang members roamin' the halls. But I still found some cool people to hang out with and smoke a little weed before class.

In the meantime, momma was spendin' almost all her time tryin' to play peacemaker between me and Todd and I could see her nerves were pretty much shot but I didn't care. She should have never taken his side. That's where she messed up. She knows me, knows how I am, and she should have never let him just come in here givin' orders and tryin' to rehab us when there was nothing wrong with us to begin with 'cept that both of us liked our weed. What Todd didn't know was that ever since I was a little kid my teacher's used to always say the same thing. They always said that I was disrespectful or had a bad attitude but momma always ignored what they had to say. She always took my side and would usually say somethin' like. 'I used to be the same way when I was growing up'. So I don't know why she figured I was gonna change for her or anybody else. And especially for that nigga layin' the pipe to her. *Please! What was she thinking?*

My chore list still hung up on the refrigerator door but he stopped demanding that I do them. And now that things were pretty much back to normal I just sat back and waited and listened. Well, it got to the point where that the house was a mess since I stopped cleaning up and he refused to clean up after me. Momma ended up doing all the cleaning just like before Todd got here and he got to feeling bad that she had to come home after workin' hard all day and then clean up. Sometimes he would try to lend a hand without saying a word but I knew it was hard on him 'cause he didn't want to tell her how to run her house anymore than he already was. And he sure didn't wanna refer to his own kids and make her think hers weren't shit or worth a damn but I could see he was havin' a hard time tryin' to understand why she was cookin' and cleanin' and mowin' the grass when there was a six-foot three, three hundred and something pound man sittin' in front of the television, eatin' and droppin' crumbs on the floor while she was tryin' to vacuum around me.

I could almost see the wheels turnin' in his head and I knew he wanted to grab her ass and call her a fat, stupid, bitch for doin' the shit I should have been doin' but instead he just left.

Now I'm figurin' that I finally got rid of him and I'm ready to celebrate a job well done but in an hour or so he was back. I think he went out and got high or drunk or somethin' crazy 'cause he just couldn't understand that this is just how we was. No crazy, high falutin' ideas about college and careers or greatness or none of that shit.

All we basically do is eat and watch TV. That's it. Nothin' more and nothin' less. Just chillin' and havin' a good time. But me loungin' around was really getting' to him 'cause all he kept sayin' was, there's nothin' worse in life than wasted time and wasted potential, whatever the hell that means.

AF Brown
Brown, Bertrand E.
Choices :

2013-11-25   APL

DATE DUE

FEB 2 5 2014			
		WITHDRAWN	
			PRINTED IN U.S.A.

Made in the USA
Lexington, KY
04 November 2013